MW00977834

RE-ROUTING

How Not to Get Lost on Life's Journey

Aunt Lori

authorHOUSE®

AuthorHouse™
1663 Liberty Drive
Bloomington, IN 47403
www.authorhouse.com
Phone: 1 (800) 839-8640

Published by AuthorHouse 09/26/2015

Library of Congress Control Number: 2015908255

ISBN: 978-1-5049-1434-5 (sc)
ISBN: 978-1-5049-1435-2 (hc)
ISBN: 978-1-5049-1436-9 (e)

Print information available on the last page.

This book is printed on acid-free paper.

Contents

Author's Note

To my parents who led by example; my children who inspired me; my grandchildren who give unconditional love; all others who taught me life lessons along the way (whether they intended to or not). The following poems are dedicated to the people that have had the most profound impacts on my life.

To My Mom

You did not lie down
when the Lion tried to attack.
Instead, you were courageous:
you leapt on his back.

You rode him fearlessly,
while surrounded by strife.
You held on, steadfast,
for the ride of your life.

Your humility belies a hero,
whom none would see.
But, you will always be
a hero to me.

To My Dad
You showed me how to navigate—
how to avoid the swales and waves—

to steer clear of trouble
and fend off the knaves.

You showed me how to use what I have,
and do what I can,
to always do better,
and try again and again.

On the exterior, you were hard as nails.
A noble man who really cared.
Then you were tired and forlorn.
You paid the price for what you dared.

I saw you in pain and suffering
then get old and frail.
You were tenacious until the end.
Even then, you did not fail.

To My Son
You are a fighter, a warrior, a king.
Your goodness is genuine and true.
Your motives divinely supreme—
if only more were just like you.

I look at you with pride.
"What a great man," I say,
"In whom many disappointments reside."
Peace be with you, I pray.

Your character is strong.
Integrity you have; all can see.
Your word many can count on.
Oh, what a blessing to me.

Your wisdom is much,
as if you were old.

Your strength is amazing,
and your love overflows.

You have persevered and you have endured—
for this you have won.
Your children will be proud,
as I am proud to call you my son.

To My Daughter
You make me proud
whenever people say
how beautiful you are.
It touches my heart in a special way.

You *are* beautiful,
both inside and out.
You're the reason I know
what life is really about.

Your elegance is understated,
your intelligence sublime.
Your kindness is to be envied;
I am proud to say you're mine.

The love I have for you,
one cannot measure.
Like the sky with its stars,
You always bring me such pleasure.

Your smile is disarming;
anyone can see.
I am happy to have you
as a part of me.

Introduction

Life's journey is an arduous one. Life is generally difficult, but it doesn't have to be. Also, you don't know and understand what you need to in order to navigate life's journey successfully. This book is about solving any problem, transcending any adverse condition, tragedy, loss, suffering—anything. It's also about love, inner strength, peace of mind, hope, miracles, and encouragement.

Everyone wants more out of life. This book will help you achieve these aspirations. With this book you can start changing your life today. It contains invaluable, pragmatic lessons that can be applied throughout your entire lifetime. It is based on the fundamental axiom that the way you think, feel, and believe determines how your life will be. You can create the life you want by following the principles contained in this book.

The knowledge and wisdom shared with you in this book is to help guide you successfully through life's journey. This book encompasses life lessons, wisdom, and reflections from many great philosophy, psychology, sociology, and science-of-mind scholars, and other great luminaries. The information is organized in a concise, cohesive, and practical way. After you have read this book you will be confident in successfully navigating life's journey.

You can have success, wealth, and anything else you want, using the teachings and techniques outlined in this book. The author shows you how to access the infinite power you already possess. It will give you insight into what's been holding you back from success. You can use the knowledge contained in this book to indoctrinate yourself and your children with the methodology of achieving success in life. It is never too early or too late to learn these doctrines. This book can be read to and by children, and is also advantageous for teenagers and senior citizens. Because we are all one, and are all connected to each other, it is the author's aim to help others' life journey become less difficult and more fulfilling.

The chapters are interrelated. Thus, reading the entire book will enhance your understanding. After you have read this book in its entirety, you may use it as a guide to solving specific problems. If you have a problem, or need guidance or inspiration, you can use this book as an intuitive conduit. You must first quiet your mind, meditate on the issue, and then ask God to show you where to start. Then randomly open this book to any page. Your answer, your direction, your guidance, your inspiration, and your encouragement will be on that page or in the section that page belongs to. Sometimes the revelation will be clear but sometimes it will be open to interpretation. It may be literal or it may be metaphorical. You must listen to your inner voice. Sometimes what you read will simply stimulate your subconscious mind to find the solution to a problem. This methodology is based on the concept that your subconscious mind can connect through its energy to a meaningful coincidence. We call this synchronicity.

The author has included poems that were inspired by circumstances and ordeals in her own life and the lives of others. All of them pertain to life and life lessons that instill encouragement, strength, inner peace, and hope.

Dive deep into the murkiness of the uncertain
and the eeriness of the unknown.
Dive deep to retrieve the revered oyster,
then swim fervently upwards toward the light.

It's the Law

$E=mc^2$ (Energy equals mass times the speed of light squared). Although it represents the theory of relativity, this equation shows the relationship between energy and matter. It helped prove that energy and matter are not separate, but different forms of the same thing. Furthermore, that we can take energy and turn it into matter, and vice versa.

Everything is energy:

- Cosmos
- Universe
- Galaxy
- Earth
- Individuals
- Organ systems
- Cells
- Molecules
- Atoms
- Subatomic particles

Albert Einstein's $E=mc^2$ proves that all things, broken down to their most elemental form, contain the same thing: energy. This one energy makes up all things, including physical entities, nature, feelings, and spirit.

The scientific field of quantum physics supports the universal law that everything that exists in the universe, at its most basic level, is essentially energy vibrating on a particular frequency. This energy is attracted to other energies on the same frequency to manifest what we experience in the physical world.

The laws of physical existence that explain energy, light, vibration, and motion have a parallel spiritual law that explains spiritual manifestation. Therefore, the principles of $E=mc^2$ are the same principles that govern the universe. Universal law embodies the concept that the universe is comprised of one collective mind. Furthermore, this collective mind is infinite and represents God. God is within us, and flows throughout everything in the universe. This means that we have the power of the infinite mind and infinite manifestation at our disposal. This also means that everything we do, say, and think impacts the universe and therefore other people and things. Universal laws assert that the spiritual universe transmutes itself through thought, which then manifests into physical substance. Therefore these universal laws, if applied correctly, will result in what you desire: success, prosperity, happiness, fulfillment, enlightenment, and so forth.

This may sound a bit like something out of Star Trek, but scientists have discovered that this energy behaves according to an individual's thoughts and beliefs. In other words, it is the individual's way of thinking and believing that determines what the energy will physically transform into. This revelation arises from Quantum Physics – Our mind creates and governs our realm of matter. There are two dominant universal laws that underlie the principle that our thoughts are creative. These are the law of attraction and the law of cause and effect.

Everything is produced by thought.

The Law of Attraction

The spiritual law of attraction is the principle that we create the circumstances, people, things and events that come into our lives. That what you are thinking about, you are attracting to you. In other words: like attracts like, and like produces like. For example, thoughts of prosperity attract prosperity to you. Conversely, thoughts of poverty attract poverty to you.

The law of attraction is believed to have its roots in ancient Greece, and it has been postulated throughout the ages. This law is also supported by science, in particular quantum physics. Quantum physics is the science of analyzing things that are experienced in life in a variety of forms and tracing them back to where they originated and were derived from, which is energy. Quantum theorists have postulated that everything that exists in our world once existed as a wave (thought), and through individual perception and expectancy was transmuted into physical form, based only on what the individual thought and believed it would appear as. If you get this, you should have goose bumps right now. This is where the law of attraction and the law of cause and effect merge (see below). These laws support the premise that our thoughts are creative, and that they create reality, including physical form. What has been discovered through quantum physics is the same law that spiritual and religious leaders have been teaching for thousands of years.

The law of attraction corresponds to and is supported by the scientific principle of the law of vibration. The law of vibration asserts that everything in the universe—including thought—has its own unique vibrational frequency. This signifies that our thoughts are on a certain vibrational frequency and ergo are part of the vibrating universe. Accordingly, positive energies attract positive energies and negative energies attract negative energies. This means that you can attract to you what you desire. It also means that you can attract to you that which you do not desire. It signifies that your life is your life because of the images and thoughts you hold in your mind. This is why it is so important to get rid of negative thoughts.

You become what you think about most.

You attract what you think about most.

There are various reasons why the law of attraction doesn't work properly for everyone, and everyone doesn't get what they want. Sending out the right thoughts and vibrations is not enough. Your positive, creative thought must coordinate with your feelings, beliefs, and actions. In other words, it is not enough to claim it. You must have feelings, beliefs and actions consistent with your thoughts. In addition to belief in the thing wished for, you must specifically believe in the universe (the power of your infinite mind) to deliver.

Any and all mental activity is not thought or thinking. Although it is difficult to define thought, it has been defined as the product of thinking. Thinking has been defined as the state of being conscious of something—to hold an idea in your mind. By positive thinking we determine what we want our lives to be. This is so because consciousness produces matter and life. Matter and life do not create consciousness, as widely thought in the past.

"Judge not, and ye shall not be judged: condemn not, and ye shall not be condemned: forgive, and ye shall be forgiven." — Luke 6:37

The law of attraction also declares that the way you think, feel, and act toward others will have a boomerang effect on you. This is because your mind is a creative intermediary. Thus what you think or feel about another, you are bringing to pass in your own life. This is also the reason why how you react to what is said or done to you is far more significant than what the person actually said or did to you. If you are kind and compassionate to others, others will be kind and compassionate to you. If you give generously to others, you will receive generously. If you give money away, you will receive more money. Conversely if you judge another, you will be judged; if you condemn another, you will be condemned, and if you do not forgive another, you will not be forgiven.

The Law of Cause and Effect

The spiritual law of cause and effect, in its simplest form means nothing happens by chance. The law of cause and effect asserts that *all* actions have reciprocal consequences. In other words, for every outcome (effect) in your life, there is a preceding cause, based on specific action or inaction on your part. Although the law of attraction and the law of cause and effect are separate distinct laws, they are similar in principle. Both assert that the way your life is—your conditions and your experiences—are a direct result of how you think and believe, whether consciously or unconsciously.

In applying both laws effectively, you must be cognizant of other principles. Firstly, the principle of oneness, which predicates that everything and everyone in the universe is interconnected. That God (the universe, supreme being, etc.) is within us, and thus we are one with God. Everything we think, believe, say, or do has a bearing upon others and the universe around us. Resultantly, whatever you do to another person, you also do to yourself and to God. This is why you should allow others to be themselves without judgment. Other people are who, what, and how they are as God made them. Just like you are who, what, and how you are, as God made you. If others are different from you, accept them and respect their differences. *Different* does not mean *worse* or *less*. It simply means different, no better, no worse. We are all the same spiritually, as we are all one. Therefore, love others as you love yourself and as God loves you.

The second principle is that gratitude is a major driving force behind getting what you want out of life. If you are appreciative and thankful for everything in your life, as well as expressing gratitude in advance for what you want, more good will happen in your life.

Thirdly, embedded in the law of cause and effect is the principle of compensation. This principle is grounded in the concept of dualism. This dualism characterizes the nature and condition of man. That is, there is always a balancing of equities in every aspect of life. For instance, for everything you have lost, you will gain something in its place; for everything you gain, you will lose something else; every excess causes a shortage. Furthermore, this purports that every good deed is rewarded and every wrong is atoned. I interpret this to mean, you pay for what you get and you get what you pay for.

Implicitly, for every benefit you receive, you have to pay it back in some manner. This edict underlies the mandate, "Pay it forward," which maintains that when we are blessed, we must bless others. We must "pay it forward" to somebody, quickly, and in the same measure. Therefore, the more blessings you confer on others, the more you will be blessed. This also means, if you gain any good thing, you must pay for it in some manner, and if you lose any good thing, you will gain some other good thing in its place. Categorically, a person who has been blessed, but doesn't bless others, will inevitably pay for it. Equivalently, if you do wrong, you will suffer for that wrong. This is referred to as retribution. Many times we are not able to witness the retribution, so we think the wrong doer has gotten away with the wrong without retribution. Whether we witness it or not, the wrong doers will pay, as there will be retribution in some way at some time. As Ralph Waldo Emerson so aptly put it:

"Every act rewards itself, or, in other words integrates itself, in a twofold manner; first in the thing, or in real nature; and secondly in the circumstance, or in apparent nature. Men call the circumstance the retribution. The causal retribution is in the thing and is seen by the soul. The retribution in the circumstance is seen by the understanding; It is inseparable from the thing, but is often spread over a long time and so does not become distinct until after many years. The specific stripes may follow late after the offence, but they follow because they accompany it. Crime and punishment grow out of one stem. Punishment is a fruit that unsuspected ripens within the flower of the pleasure that concealed it. Cause and effect, means and ends, seed and fruit, cannot be severed; for the effect already blooms in the cause, the end preexists in the means, the fruit in the seed" —Ralph Waldo Emerson, *Compensation*

> "Give, and it shall be given unto you; good measure, pressed
> down, and shaken together, and running over, shall men give

into your bosom. For with the same measure that ye mete withal it shall be measured to you again." —Luke 6:38

Fourthly, the principle of giving and receiving pronounces that in order to receive something you must give something to others. Reciprocally, you get what you desire by helping others get what they desire. Giving and receiving is an integral part of the universe. However, you must feel that you deserve to receive something in return for giving something. Oftentimes low self-esteem and the absence of self-love makes us feel we do not deserve to receive anything in exchange for giving to others. Erroneously we think that there is a shortage of wealth and prosperity in the universe. In fact, the Universe is infinitely wealthy, and there is more than enough for everyone.

Giving and receiving guidelines:

- Give so that others can receive, and so you can be compensated for your giving;
- Presume that you deserve to be compensated for your giving;
- Expect to be compensated for your giving;
- Welcome good things that come to you, and do not question your good fortune.

Finally, getting what you want out of life doesn't end with knowing and applying the laws. To benefit from the laws, you may need to take some type of action. Therefore, in addition to thinking and believing, identify the things you need to do to get the desired result (effect), and then take action. Above all, persevere in your thinking and belief.

Following the aforementioned laws and principles will help you transcend to greater enlightenment on your spiritual journey through life. Enlightenment is really the reason our spirit manifests as physical beings on earth. Life on earth is meant to be a journey, whereby we experience life and learn lessons as we head toward enlightenment as our destination. Enlightenment is essentially the concept of being spiritually and consciously aware. It consists of recognizing the oneness of the universe and that consciousness is our true nature. It can be thought of as the product of spiritual growth. Highly evolved souls are considered enlightened.

Everything Is Relative

"Everything is relative" refers to the principle that everything is made real only by its relationship or comparison to something else. For instance, light exists because we compare it to darkness; hot exists because we compare it to cold, and so forth. Moreover, the meaning or value that something has for us is the meaning or value we give it, based on relating it to something or comparing it to something else.

Whenever you compare your physical life to someone else's, your life will look better or worse, depending on whose life you're using for comparison. You may look at and compare your life to Oprah Winfrey's apparent physical life and say, "My life sucks." On the other hand, if you look at and compare your life to a homeless person's, you might say, "My life is good". Accordingly, when we view our problems we must see them in proper perspective. Therefore if we compare our problems with greater problems, ours doesn't seem so bad. If we compare our problems to lesser problems, however, our problems will seem worse.

Problems, trouble, and challenges should all be viewed as opportunities for advancement and learning. In life, we are all faced with a series of problems, trouble, and challenges as tests. In order to address these problems we must first put them in proper perspective. We must be mindful that no matter how difficult we perceive our circumstances to be, there is always someone who is in a worse position.

When trouble comes into your life, the manner in which you deal with it is important. How you deal with it is largely based on which thoughts and perspective you use to think about the problem. Is the glass half empty or half full? The truth is, if you focus on the good in any circumstance, more good will come to you. It is equally true that if you focus on how bad your circumstances are, you will attract more bad to you.

For instance, take two children who grow up in the same dysfunctional home, both deprived of the same comforts of life. Both are abused by the same parent. However, one sees his life as really terrible. Consequently he focuses on how bad his life is and what he doesn't have. This negative thinking leads him to feel sorry for himself, and he becomes an addict. This only serves to compound his problems. In order to feed his addiction he steals and robs people, which ultimately lands him in prison. The other child, on the other hand, saw how poverty and dysfunctional circumstances were affecting the people around him. Once he made the determination that his life could be worse, he resolved that he would be grateful for what he had and would seek out the positive things in his life. Once he realized that the glass was half full, he knew life could be better. Consequently he soaked in all the knowledge that he could, and he decided education would be the way to enhance his dismal life. As a result he attained an MBA and started a highly lucrative business. The difference in how these brothers' lives turned out started with how they perceived their lives and the world they lived in. Negative feelings like pity, resentment, hatred, and self-loathing can only serve to attract more negativity into one's life.

It is not our circumstances; instead, it is our perception of
our circumstances that determine our power to change them.

You've Fallen and You Can Get Up—Trouble in Life

We all encounter trouble in our lives. What determines the outcome of trouble is how we deal with it. The key to successfully dealing with trouble, problems, challenges, trials, and disappointments is to have a positive reaction to them. You shouldn't be afraid of the dark, as you shouldn't be afraid of trouble. Much the same as dark transforms into light, trouble ends.

In order to fix anything that is broken, you must first acknowledge that it is in fact broken. Many people suffer far too long, live in denial for far too long, and do not grow because they are stuck. They are stuck because they do not acknowledge they are broken. If you do not acknowledge something is broken, it is almost impossible to fix it. Another way to view what is broken is to view it as a problem.

To find strength, we must first admit weakness.

If you have a broken heart, whether because your husband left you for a younger woman after twenty-five years of marriage, or you walked in on the love of your life having sex with your best friend, or the person you trusted the most stole from you, you have a broken heart. It is a problem if you don't realize it's a problem. There can be many detrimental effects of a broken heart, such as unwillingness to trust again, hatred, resentment, depression, and neurosis.

Broken dreams, unfulfilled dreams, or deferred dreams can be devastating and can lead to a broken spirit. Many people have unfulfilled dreams. How unfulfilled dreams affect you, however, depends on how you deal with it. If you do not take it in stride, never get over it, blame others, let it eat away at you, or manifest as resentment, you will be affected negatively.

"Everything will be all right in the end. If it's not all right, it's not the end." —Unknown

A broken spirit may manifest itself in feelings of hopelessness and depression. Many people are carrying around massive amounts of emotional pain and find life difficult. Their future may look dismal or they may feel there is no way out of their troubles. Perhaps the loss of a loved one precipitated these feelings. Perhaps they are carrying around a lot of unresolved hurt and pain. Invasive negative thoughts can make troubles seem impossible to get rid of. There is always a way out. In fact, in all circumstances you can think your way out of your troubles, whether it's overwhelming financial troubles, impending tragedy, or a life threatening situation.

"This too shall pass. " —Unknown

There was a woman that I counseled, who was a teacher. She was also married to a teacher. As it turned out, this woman's husband was a covert drug dealer. She was unaware of this. She knew something was not quite right, because he spent a lot more money than he made. She never really questioned him, because she was benefiting from the excess money as well. She was never involved in her husband's activities in any way. She was consumed with working and taking care of her three children. One fateful day her husband called her and asked her to give a package to a friend that was stopping by to pick it up. The friend came to her home, and she handed over the package. Much to her shock and dismay, the friend turned out to be an undercover police officer. She was arrested on the spot and taken from her home, and she would not see her young children again for many years. Her husband claimed that he did not know anything about the drugs, and was given immunity to testify against her. She was subsequently sentenced to five years in prison. She appealed, lost the appeal, and was re-sentenced to ten years. Her husband did not visit her in prison, and he would not bring her children to visit. This woman had dreams of getting her PhD, becoming a principal, and eventually school superintendant.

She also had dreams of seeing her children grow up. When I met her, her spirit was broken. She suffered from depression and was on medication. Because of what happened to her, she lost hope. Resentment became a part of her and crippled her spiritually. Living in the past, she was consumed with self-pity. She was barely able to function and living each day was a challenge. Everyday of her life was inundated with the question, why me? I explained to her that her situation wouldn't last forever. She had to find some way to reach deep inside and find the courage and the strength to pick up the broken pieces and salvage her life. I was able to get across to her that life is what you make of it. She need only make the decision to be happy and free from depression. I explained the steps necessary to achieve this, which I explain in this book. Consequently, she decided to move forward, start living her life, and to trust God. She used the time in prison to study, and completed her PhD after she was released. She was reunited with her children and regained custody when her husband was caught dealing drugs and sent to prison.

Life is fraught with trouble. In life the issue is not will trouble come, but when will it come. It will come. Trouble oftentimes results in a broken heart, broken dreams, or a broken spirit. Trouble can manifest itself in negative ways if you allow it to. Having a happy, fulfilled life is not about the absence of trouble. It's about how you deal with trouble when it does come.

> "That then the Lord thy God will turn thy captivity, and have compassion upon thee, and will return and gather thee from all the nations, wither the Lord thy God hath scattered thee. If any of thine be driven out unto the outmost parts of heaven, from thence will the Lord thy God gather thee, and from thence will he fetch thee: And the Lord thy God will bring thee into the land which thy fathers possessed, and thou shalt possess it; and he will do thee good, and multiply thee above thy fathers. And the Lord thy God will circumcise thine heart, and the heart of thine seed, to love the Lord thy God with all thine heart, and with all thy soul, that thou mayest live." –Deuteronomy 30:3-6

Life is always changing. Trouble doesn't last forever. No matter what happens in your life, know that God will restore whatever you've lost. No matter how bad things get, you can pick up the pieces and have a good life.

Living your life successfully is fundamentally about how you handle or react to trouble and challenges. When life gets rough, and tough times seem like they will never end, and your dreams seem like they will never come true, hold on. We oftentimes cannot control situations that we find ourselves in; however, we can control our perceptions and reactions to them. Don't get discouraged and give up. Life follows your thoughts and beliefs, not the other way around. So, when you fall down, believe that you can get up. Then get up!

Pay Now or Pay Later

You can't run and you can't hide from trouble. You must learn to face trouble head on. Do not run from it. If you run from it, it will only get worse and hurt you more. You have the power to transcend your troubles by viewing them as opportunities to grow spiritually stronger and wiser.

> You gain strength not in the absence of trouble, but when trouble strangles you, and you look it in the eye, rise above it, and choke back.

Sometimes decisions are difficult to make. Sometimes the most important decision you can make is the one to make a decision. Make a decision to do the thing you have been afraid or reluctant to do. If you don't pay the cost of making a decision sooner rather than later, you will end up paying far more later. If you fail to make a decision, the decision will be made for you. If you fall off a horse, will you lie there and wait to see what the horse is going to do?

If you are in business and you are struggling financially, you may need to make the decision to close your doors, cut your losses, and re-group. Don't wait until the landlord evicts you. I have been a business owner my whole adult life. Overall I have been very successful. However, there were a few times when I had to make the difficult decision to close down and cut my losses. I never missed a beat. I got right back up, salvaged what I could, and started rebuilding. Having a failing business is like falling out of a boat into a lake. If you stay calm, you can start swimming back to the shore. On the other hand if you keep holding on to the cap-sized boat, it will take you longer to recover, and you may never recover.

It's a Mind Game

Once you have determined that you need to change for the better. How do you specifically go about making that change? To change your circumstances, your life, or the person you are, you must first change your thinking. Realize that the world you live in is determined largely by what goes on in your mind. You can literally *think* the life you want into existence. Until your thought changes, your conditions never will.

"A man's life is what his thoughts make of it." —Marcus Aurelius

The thought or word that you think or speak today is the law that will control your life tomorrow. The thought or word you thought or spoke yesterday, ignorantly or innocently, intentionally or unintentionally, is controlling your life today. As long as you claim less, you will get less. You will get what you think about.

If you think or say:

"I am broke," you are creating more financial loss;
"I am sick," you are creating more illness;
"I am depressed," you are creating more despair;
"I am lonely," you are creating more loneliness;
"I am unhappy," you are creating more unhappiness.

Get the picture? Your life—the things and people you create into your reality—mirrors what you believe subconsciously. There is a cognitive cause for everything. Behind every problem, there is a definite cause. If you are sick, have insomnia, are impoverished, overweight, unmotivated, or mentally ill–the cause of the problem is something negative like fear, doubt, hate, confusion, un-forgiveness, or disbelief. To overcome these and any other problems, you need to constantly think them away with the opposite positive thought. Repetitively think over and over what you want or what you want to happen, because what you think about the most is what will happen. Constantly think thoughts of peace, happiness, forgiveness, confidence, love, prosperity, and faith. You have the power to change anything, because you can choose your thoughts. Therefore, you can create your own reality.

Our feelings let us know what we are thinking. Our thoughts are cause, and our feelings are effect. Positive feelings make you feel good, and negative feelings make you feel bad. If you are feeling bad then you are having thoughts that make you feel bad. Unfortunately when you are feeling bad, you effectually attract more bad consequences to you.

There is an infinite power within you. Good things like happiness, success, and prosperity will come to you when you have unwavering confidence in this power. The power of manifestation is the power to willfully create anything you desire into reality. This power is generated by your subconscious mind.

Reminders to effectively transmute thoughts into reality (substance):

- Your thoughts, words, feelings, beliefs, affirmations, visualizations, goals, and actions must be aligned with the thing you desire and wish to manifest;
- You must have a prophetic crystal clear vision of what you desire;
- You must maintain your focus and continually direct your thoughts and feelings toward the thing desired;
- You must be prepared to do whatever act might be necessary to facilitate the manifestation;
- You must expect complete success;
- You must believe: "believing is seeing" *not* "seeing is believing";
- It is not enough to have positive thoughts in your conscious mind; the positive thoughts must be embedded in your subconscious mind;

- Whatever your conscious mind assumes and believes to be true, your subconscious mind will accept and bring to pass;
- Ideas can be conveyed to your subconscious mind by repetition, faith, and expectancy;
- Every achievement was first projected as a creative idea;
- You can do anything through the power of your subconscious mind.

Not using your infinite power of manifestation is like having a humongous lake in your backyard and dying of thirst.

Affirmations

Affirmations are repetitive thoughts in the form of *positive* statements of what you would like to manifest. They are used to reprogram your subconscious mind from negative thoughts to positive thoughts.

You must be very careful how you phrase your affirmations. They must be affirmative. This means that you cannot continuously think thoughts like, "I don't want to be poor," as you are still attracting poverty. This is because your subconscious mind cannot make a distinction between, "I don't want to be poor" and, "I want to be poor". In this exemplification, your subconscious mind only picks up "poor". Consequently, the very thing that you don't want is what you are attracting to you. This is a significant but subtle caveat of the law of attraction. For this reason, you have to be mindful of how you think and express your affirmations. To reiterate, your subconscious mind cannot discern a negative expression from a positive expression. Accordingly, negative words like *can't*, *won't*, and *don't* bring the very situation or thing to you that you do not want. In conclusion, only think in positive terminologies, like, "I am wealthy". Affirmations must also be expressed in the present tense, presuming that you already have what you desire. Remember, if you consciously assume something is true, your subconscious mind will accept it as true and proceed to manifest it.

Improper affirmations:	Proper affirmations:
I am not sick.	I am in perfect health.
I am not poor.	Prosperity is mine now.

I am not afraid.	Peace and courage govern my mind at all times.
I don't want to be mean.	I am a kind and loving person.
I don't want to be sad.	I choose happiness everyday.
I want to believe in myself.	I believe in myself and the power of my infinite mind.
I am not ugly.	I am beautiful and desirable.
I am not dumb.	I am smart and resourceful.
I am free of drugs in my life.	Only things that are pure and good for me are in my life.
I don't want to feel frustrated and defeated.	I believe that all things are possible.
I don't want to be fat.	My body is in perfect condition.
I don't want to lose my memory.	My memory is in perfect working order.
I want my cancer to go away.	Every organ and cell in my body is functioning perfectly.
I want to change my bad habits.	I can do all things through the infinite power of my subconscious mind.

In order to perpetuate your manifestation, continue making affirmations even after you have manifested your thoughts into reality. Allegorically, if it doesn't rain over a period of time, a drought will result. Always show gratitude for what you already have and give thanks in advance for what you want. You will find additional sample affirmations later on in this book.

Creative Visualization

Creative visualization is a fundamental technique underlying the manifestation of your desires into reality. It is using the power of your imagination to picture in your mind's eye what you desire, or what you want to become. This imaging has the effect of creating and attracting what you desire.

You are perpetually creating your life by the thoughts fixated in your mind and your imagination. Use creative visualization to attract what you want. Visualization entails creating a picture in your mind of what you want or what you want to be and generating feelings of already having or being it. You have to see and feel it. If you want a new home, you have to see it in your mind exactly as you want it, and feel yourself in the home.

Creative visualization is typically a three step process: 1) invoke imagination; 2) invoke feelings; 3) invoke the power of belief. Before commencing the creative visualization process, you must get yourself in a relaxed state, as you would to meditate (see Meditation section).

Creative visualization is generally more powerful than affirmations. It is essentially imagination, using your power of thought to create a mental image of what you desire or what you want to become. In other words, you create vivid pictures in your mind of what you want to manifest in your physical life.

Tips to effectuate the power of creative visualization:

- In a relaxed state, close your eyes and visualize what you desire or how you wish to see yourself.

- Focus on what you want. Similar to effectively using affirmations, don't think in negative terms, as in what you don't want. Focus on seeing precisely what you want from a positive viewpoint.
- Create the images in your mind as though you are viewing a movie (with you in it). For instance, see yourself driving the Mercedes you want, moving into the house you want, living in the new house, and so forth. Use all of your senses in your creative visualizations. See, hear, touch, taste, and smell what you desire in this movie in your mind.
- Imagine what you want in the present moment, not in the future; view it as though you have it now.
- Get into the habit of practicing creative visualization on a regular basis. Make it a part of your daily routine. The creative power of your visualizations is determined in large part by repetitiveness.
- Combine your creative visualization sessions with your meditation and affirmation sessions. Meditate prior to commencing the creative visualization process, as this will clear your mind and make it more receptive.
- Using a vision board may aid creative visualization. A vision board is comprised of pictures that signify all the things you want to attract to you. For example, you may have pictures of the car and type house you desire, the type clothes you want to wear, the office you want, the boat, and so on. The vision board is intended to reinforce your competency to manifest your vision. It also acts to inspire you to stay the course.
- Actually experience as many of the things you desire, as this will heighten the feelings associated with the experience, and make it easier to invoke the requisite feelings. For instance, test drive the car you desire. Make an appointment to tour some houses similar to the type you desire.
- If you wish to manifest wealth or prosperity, fill out a check and mail it to yourself. Fill in the desired amount: one million? Ten million? One hundred million? More? It's up to you. Wealth is unlimited, and there's more than enough to go around.

Invoke feelings in your imagination by reacting to the images in the same manner as you would react when they manifest in your life. Invoke feelings like pleasure, excitement, love, happiness, gratitude, and joy. When you combine your mental images with positive feelings, you magnify the creative power of your thoughts. For example, experience happiness. Be sure to invoke the feelings of love, gratitude, and peace. Feel love because it demonstrates self-love and internalizes the idea that you deserve to receive that which you desire. Love also exemplifies the concept that you are one with God (the universe), which is the source of all love. Feel gratitude for all that you have in your life, in addition to that which you will receive. Lastly, invoke the feeling of peace and know that everything is manifesting in divine order. Know that regardless of what is currently happening in your life, it can and will change through the power of your mind.

Believe that your desires have already been manifested without a doubt. If you truly understand the truth about the power of your mind to manifest your desires, then you will believe it. If you do not truly believe, you may use affirmations to help you believe.

After completing the process, let go and leave the rest up to God (the universe). Don't question whether what you visualized will show up. Be at peace knowing that your imagination is unlimited, as is your infinite power to create that which you desire.

Meditation

"Be still, and know that I *am* God" —Psalm 46:10

Prayer is used to talk to God. Meditation can be used to listen to God and communicate with God (the universe). To listen, your mind must be still. When you are still your spirit is more energetic and focused. Meditation is a way to quiet and renew the mind. It is also a means to induce feelings of love and peace and to receive guidance. You must set aside time to listen. When you take time to listen to God, you're taking time for yourself. Negative thoughts may preclude us from hearing from God (the universe). Whenever you feel negative thoughts interfering, recite inwardly, "Peace be with me."

To meditate is to think, to contemplate, to ponder. There are many types of meditation. It is basically a way to control one's thoughts. It involves clearing the mind of negative or unwanted thoughts. It may involve the repetition of affirmations as a way of training the mind to think positively. Meditation has side effects of reducing stress and anxiety. It is recommended that you take the time to meditate daily.

Tips on how to meditate:

- Change into comfortable clothes;
- Make sure your location is quiet, free of distractions, and at a comfortable temperature;
- Turn off your cell phone;
- Sit in a comfortable chair or lie on the floor or bed. Sitting comfortably in a chair is preferable, as you're not as susceptible

to falling asleep as you would be lying down. It is best to locate yourself where you don't normally work or do other activities like watch TV;

- Be still and quiet; close your eyes;
- Forget the activities of the day;
- Rid your mind of any mental, physical, or emotional problems;
- Relax your body. There are a number of ways to relax, such as counting backwards. I prefer to concentrate on my breathing, which is the best way to relax. Take deep breaths, inhaling through your nose. Breathe deeply, so you feel the air in your lungs. Hold your breath momentarily, and then exhale slowly through your mouth. Contract your stomach when you inhale, and release your stomach when you exhale. Remember to continue breathing deeply for the duration of your meditation period;
- Relax all your muscles and float;
- Imagine the sun shining on your face, then imagine it moving slowly down your body;
- Focus your attention. Lighting a candle and making it your focal point may help;
- Hold a thought or problem in your mind for which you are seeking guidance. Wait for it, the answer will come;
- Repeat affirmations silently, positively, and in the present tense;
- Schedule meditation time into your daily routine. Twenty minutes two times a day is ideal. First thing upon rising and last thing before bed is advantageous.

Who Are You?

You must see yourself clearly as you are before you can change. Self-concept refers to how we think about or perceive ourselves. The self-concept is also how we evaluate ourselves.

Influential psychologist, Carl Rogers, delineates self-concept into three parts:

1. The view you have of yourself (self-image);
2. How much value you place on yourself (self-esteem or self-worth);
3. What you wish you were really like (ideal self).

One issue with the self-concept is that one's image does not necessarily reflect reality. Charles H. Cooley developed the social psychological concept of "the looking glass self". This concept espouses that our self-image is based on how we think others see us. He also states that we perceive how others see us and make judgments about us, and we form our identity based on these perceptions. Moreover, when we encounter other people important to us, who view us differently, we may change our identity or self-concept. Furthermore, we may also keep changing our self-concept throughout life.

Another issue with the self-concept is that our self-image is not congruent with what we wish we were really like. Examples of these types of incongruences are:

- You cannot keep a man because you are filled with resentment and loathing because a man hurt you deeply in the past. You

are self-centered and selfish. You're really not happy being a self-centered, self-absorbed, and unpleasant person. You would like to be a kind, compassionate, and loving partner to a man in a sustained relationship, preferably marriage.
- You're hanging out with people that you know are losers, and you have acquired their same traits such as laziness, irresponsibility, lethargy, complacency, and mediocrity. You don't work, and you're going nowhere fast. You would like to have a job that you like, be a productive contributor to your household, and have a family of your own one day.
- You were in the wrong place at the wrong time with a friend, and due to no fault of your own, you were arrested and convicted of a crime. Your self- image and self-esteem suffered. You feel that your record has prevented you from becoming as successful as you would like. You would like to be truly positive and successful in spite of your past.

Some sociologists and psychologists theorize that the motivation for initiating cognitive and behavioral change is for the enhancement of the self-concept. This entails the methodology of self-confrontation. This involves obtaining objective feedback designed to increase self-awareness. One then sees a contradiction between one's self-conception and the objective facts about oneself. In other words what you say, believe, or do is inconsistent with your self-conception. This leads to self–dissatisfaction, which in turn initiates a process of cognitive and behavioral change. Take a look at the behaviors that got you where you are and that are holding you back from getting to where you want to go.

Denial and projection hinder change and self-improvement. The psychological and spiritual concept of projection is a defense mechanism. We place (or project) our own undesirable qualities, traits, or feelings onto other people. These undesirable qualities, traits, or feelings are displaced onto another person in order to create an external threat and avoid examining any internal threats. For example, you strongly dislike someone because of a certain negative trait, yet you deny this undesirable trait in yourself. You attribute the dislike to the subject of your dislike, e.g. "She hates me." Likewise, a cheating spouse may project accusations of infidelity onto his or her spouse, so that the guilt associated with cheating can be turned to blame instead.

If you are angry and hostile, you project your anger and hostility onto others. You will perceive them as being angry and hostile towards you, whether they are or not. You will perceive anger and hostility where none was intended, and none actually shown. Those who project hatred, resentment, hostility, and rage generally think everyone is out to get them. Accordingly, if you project negative traits, qualities, and feelings onto others (traits that you yourself have), you will attract the same to you. Furthermore, projecting these negative traits, qualities and feelings will prevent you from taking responsibility for your own actions. Projection is a strong form of denial. Conversely, by projecting positive qualities, traits, or feelings towards others, you attract positive energy to you.

All change begins with acknowledgement of the situation or problem. Denial is an enormous obstacle to change. Denial doesn't help solve problems, nor do fear, hostility, blame, or resentment. People use denial in order to make unacceptable, unpleasant circumstances more acceptable. For example, individuals with an addiction subconsciously know that it is unpleasant and unacceptable. However, because they have a distorted view of reality, while in denial they cannot make the right decisions in order to make a change. For instance, alcoholics and addicts generally are in denial, as it enables them to continue their destructive habits.

In my opinion, people who need to make a change in their lives fall into one of three categories:

1. Those who are in denial;
2. Those who admit they have a problem, yet will not take the necessary steps to change;
3. Those who admit they have a problem, take steps to change, and do make a change.

Generally speaking, the difference between those in category number two and number three is belief. They do not believe they can change. They both may be motivated and incited to change, but they just don't believe they have the power to do so.

I am acquainted with individuals in all three categories. One young lady is a hard core alcoholic. She has numerous DUI convictions and gets publically intoxicated on a regular basis, usually to her detriment. She doesn't believe she is an alcoholic. She admits that she drinks a lot, but because she has a high tolerance level (in her mind), she doesn't believe she is an alcoholic. Unfortunately, it may take a very tragic situation for her to face the actual fact that she is an alcoholic engaged in destructive behavior.

Another young lady came to me in tears, admitting that she had a problem. She admitted she was an alcoholic and that she felt that drinking was doing damage to her physically. Astonishingly, her father had died relatively young from complications of the liver due to excessive drinking. I recommended that she do research and decide on a technique for dealing with her problem. I told her that it didn't matter which technique she used as long as she thought it would work, believed that she could change, and believed in the power within her to do so. Above all, she needed to take action accordingly. She hasn't been able to take the necessary steps, due basically to her lack of belief.

I also know of a man who had been a drug addict for years. At first he wouldn't admit it to himself. He finally came to the realization that he had a serious problem. Upon making this determination, he immediately took action to quit cold turkey. Without help from anyone, he was able to quit. Because he really believed that he could change, he has been drug free for more than twenty years, and he has never looked back.

Categorically, you can change *anything*. Firstly, control your thoughts. Secondly, take constructive steps that are consistent with your thoughts. Thirdly, you not only must believe that you can change but that you have the power within yourself to change.

Reinvent Yourself—Be Everything You Want to Be

"Whose adorning let it not be that outward *adorning* of plaiting the hair, and of wearing of gold, or of putting on of apparel; But *let it be* the hidden man of the heart, in that which is not corruptible, *even the ornament* of a meek and quiet spirit, which is in the sight of God of great price." —1 Peter 3:3–4

It is not your outward appearance that matters in life. It is really your inner self that is most important. You can change yourself from the inside out, and the rest will take care of itself. Start with a gentle and peaceful spirit. You can do and have and be things that you never thought possible. See yourself how and with whatever you desire. Believe that you are awesome, that there's something great about you, regardless of what has happened to you in the past, regardless of your age, and regardless of the troubles that have brought you to where you are. Believe and tap into the infinite powers within you to create the life you want and deserve. The more power you use, the more powerful you become.

"Know ye not that ye are the temple of God, and *that* the Spirit of God dwelleth in you?"—1 Cor 3:16

If you know that God's spirit lives in you, then you know that you have unlimited power. It is only your doubts, fears, lack of confidence, and low self-esteem that limit you and your potential. Whatever your situation may be, you can improve it. How you see yourself will affect your life's conditions. Don't allow low self-esteem or a negative self-image to keep you from being your best. You must see yourself as a winner to be a winner.

Thought is creative.

You can create the person you want to be if you simply believe in the power of your mind.

How to use your mind to literally create a new and improved you:

- You must convey your desires and needs to your subconscious mind, as your subconscious mind will accept what you really feel to be true, and create it in reality.
- You must use your imagination, which is your most powerful asset, as you are what you imagine yourself to be.
- Get in the habit of using positive affirmations to create desired positive results. Whenever negative thoughts enter your mind, dispel them by repeating appropriate affirmations. (These represent the opposite of your negative thought).
- You must continually think of success, prosperity, health, and happiness. By taking control of your thoughts, you will bring forth good and desirable changes within yourself and without.
- Get rid of negative people in your life.
- Utilize aids such as creative visualization and vision boards. Picture the person you want to be and the life you would like to have. Write down the description in detail. Visualize yourself as that person. Visualize yourself living that life.
- Determine how you need to change to be that person. Write down the traits or things that you don't like about yourself in one column, and write down the traits or things you wish to substitute them for in a second column. Accordingly, write down the things about your life you don't like in one column, and the things you wish to substitute in another column.
- Take leave of ordinary reality. You must take breaks and depart from the norm. Stop and take a look at the world outside yourself. Do something or explore something different. Relax and totally let go. If you're a serious person, go to a comedy club and laugh. Learn how to do something new. Take a hike—literally.

- Believe you can be the person and have the life that you want. Use the infinite powers of your mind to create a new self and a new life. This may include breaking bad habits and making major changes. Understand that you are the sum total of your thoughts, and you can substitute productive thoughts for non-productive thoughts.
- Thank God for what you have imagined and visualized.
- Take action. The combination of positive thinking, positive belief, positive affirmations, creative visualization, gratitude, expectancy, and positive action will result in actualization of what you desire.

You can always start over, right now, right where you are.

Accept You Are Number One

The most important person in your life is yourself. You must take care of yourself before you can take care of others. You must love yourself before you can love others. This means you must make decisions, based on accepting that you are number one. Acceptance of yourself as number one does not negate nor diminish your love for others in your life. Nor does it mean that you are selfish.

Many years ago I was faced with the decision to divorce my second husband. I married the first time while in college. When I divorced my first husband, I immediately got into a relationship with my second husband. I never really had time to experience freedom as an adult. I knew I'd made a mistake by marrying my second husband, and I was unhappy. What made the decision so difficult was the fact that he was a great husband and provider. He was kind and easy to get along with. I knew he really loved me, and we had a beautiful daughter together. I was still unhappy. I was into the arts, higher education, and trying new things. I was also highly ambitious and competitive. My husband was nothing like me. It wasn't long before this was a problem. I dreamed daily of being free. As a result, I couldn't eat, and I started losing weight. I was only a buck ten to start with. I felt depressed and became increasingly more depressed because I was overcome with guilt. I felt guilty because he had done nothing wrong. I decided to see a medical doctor. He said there was nothing physically wrong and asked me what was going on in my life. I told him about wanting to leave my husband and that I couldn't bring myself to do it. To this day, I remember what he said: "You're unhappy because you haven't faced your problem and made a decision. You need to get off the fence and make a decision. You need to realize that you are number one in your life, and you have to do what is best for number one, even if it hurts someone else, even if it hurts you to hurt someone else. So, you need to bite the bullet and face the dragons."

I had never thought about myself like that before. I repeated, "I am number one and I deserve to be happy," to myself over and over until I had internalized it and actually believed it. I was then able to bite the bullet and leave my husband. It still remains one of the most difficult things I've ever had to do. It broke his heart, but it freed me. When I reflect back on it, I know it was the right decision. He ended up with a great new family, and I was able to spread my wings and soar.

Believe that you deserve to be happy. If you don't believe you deserve to be happy, or have the things you desire, then you won't. You must change how you feel about yourself and consequently how you treat yourself. You cannot make someone else happy if you yourself are not happy. Similarly, you cannot love someone else until you love yourself. Make sure you put yourself first and take care of your wants and needs. Do something nice for yourself on a regular basis. For instance, designate one day a month as "my day," "whatever I want day," or "I am number one day." This will force you to put yourself first. Get rid of the kids, the husband, and the dog. This is the day that you remind yourself of how important you are and that you deserve whatever you desire.

Give Yourself a Pass

Self-acceptance is embracing all aspects of our self, the positive and the negative. It is non-judgmentally accepting who we are, with whatever strengths and weaknesses we have. We become more self-accepting by letting go of guilt, forgiving ourselves, developing self compassion, and getting over self-judgments. Self-acceptance is an integral part of self-love.

Self-acceptance asks the question, "Do I like myself"? Self-esteem asks the question, "Do I think I am valuable and worthwhile"? Self-acceptance impacts one's self-confidence and one's self-esteem. Your self-esteem and self-confidence will increase as your self-acceptance increases. Self-acceptance should not be tantamount to self-achievement. Therefore, our mistakes and failures should not be equated to who we are and how we feel about ourselves. Forgive yourself when you make a mistake. Stop judging yourself and don't measure you self-worth against other people's apparent worth. Instead focus on improving that which you don't like about yourself. If you spend your time berating yourself and beating yourself up, you won't be able to focus on growth and self-improvement.

As a general rule, we tend to develop self-acceptance similarly to the way we develop our self-esteem, that is, how we view our parent's acceptance of us. Unfortunately, the positive feedback we received from our parents probably depended entirely on how we acted. Our parents may have used negative words or actions to control us. Sadly, the import of this is that our behaviors weren't acceptable to them. Consequently, in identifying ourselves with these negative behaviors, we internalize a sense of inadequacy. In addition to this, negative parental evaluations such as, "you're selfish," "you're fat," "you're bad," may have a negative effect on a child. The child will view himself or herself negatively. I have a grandson who is a toddler. One day I said to him, "Be a good boy." He blurted, emphatically and with fervor, "I'm not a good boy." This was a real eye-opener for me, and it caused me to re-evaluate how we, as caregivers, should relate to children. Of course I shared this insight with the child's parent.

In cases where parents are too critical, the child may internalize feelings of rejection, inferiority, and low self-worth as a consequence. This parental criticism is oftentimes carried over into adulthood and generates self-criticism, which is the antithesis of self-acceptance. This leads to problems in adulthood.

There is really no true guidebook on how to parent. We can, however, read about other's experiences and be aware of how we control children. We tend to parent as we were parented. I don't have all the answers, but I have come to believe that negativity leads to negativity. So if we were berated, physically punished, and continually chastised we will tend to beat ourselves up. On the one hand, parents cannot ignore bad behavior. On the other hand, we must acknowledge the child's positive behavior and focus less on the negative behavior. Likewise, to become more accepting of yourself as an adult, focus more on your positive attributes than your negative attributes.

Self-acceptance may seem counterintuitive to self-improvement. With self-acceptance we are simply non-judgmentally recognizing and accepting who we are. Self-acceptance is important, so that we do not feel undeserving. Self-acceptance and self-improvement coexist, as self-acceptance does not in any way diminish the need for self-improvement.

Ways to develop self-acceptance:

1. Develop self-compassion;
2. Focus more on positives than negatives;
3. Forgive yourself for faults or mistakes;
4. Stop looking for approval from others;
5. Avoid self-deprecating thoughts or comments like, "I'm such an idiot"; "I'm so fat," and "I disgust myself";
6. Make a list of your strengths and weaknesses. Then decide which you want to improve upon, without guilt, shame, or beating yourself up;
7. Repeat positive affirmations about yourself.

You are not what you were in the past; you are not your mistakes; you are not your failures. You are what you have learned and what you have overcome. Let the obstacles in life show you the way to a better, future you.

Failing Doesn't Make You a Failure

Failing at something doesn't make you a failure. As a matter of fact, failure is oftentimes necessary in order to succeed. If you've failed at something, you generally will know better than someone who hasn't failed.

Experience is a good teacher, but failure is a better teacher.

You only fail if you don't try. You cannot know what the outcome of trying something might be. However, you can be certain what the outcome will be if you don't try. Unequivocally, without a doubt the outcome will be failure.

Here is a little known fact about me that my family and close friends don't even know: Back when I graduated from law school, I didn't realize that failure didn't make you a failure. I had taken the Michigan bar exam, and I failed. Because I had rarely failed at anything, I was devastated. When I received the letter that I had failed, I felt like a failure. I was so ashamed that I couldn't deal with taking the Michigan bar again. I moved to Texas, as far away from Michigan as I could get. I knew that I hadn't properly prepared for the Michigan exam, so I really prepared for the Texas exam. For many years, I pretended that I hadn't even taken the Michigan bar exam, because it was too painful to revisit. Two significant things came out of that failure. Firstly, it taught me to always be prepared. When I took the bar exam in Texas I was a lot more prepared, and I passed on the first try. Secondly, it was a way that the universe was telling me that there was something better for me elsewhere.

Learn the lessons to be learned in failure. If you don't take anything away from failure, it was for naught.

While it is unpleasant to think about past failures, you do learn from them. It is difficult to find a success story without a failure story. Failure is not a sign of inferiority; failure is crucial to success. Whenever I was hiring a new lawyer at my firm, I would always ask them about their failures as well as their successes. I knew that someone who had failed would have invaluable experience. I would always be leery of someone who said they had never had any failures. I would rather hire someone who tried and failed than someone who was not willing to take risks.

Failures only make us better.

Doubt leads to failure. Oftentimes when we experience failure, we have a tendency to doubt ourselves. Doubt is a negative emotion that generally leads straight to failure. Doubt, like all negative emotions, will make you discouraged. If you'll notice, the word *discouraged* is comprised of the word *courage*. However, it is the opposite of courage. Self-doubt produces feelings of confusion and chaos and will oftentimes lead to inaction. Inaction that is tantamount to failure.

When faced with doubt, stop and take deep breaths. Think about something that represents a strength or a positive action you can do instead. Whenever you feel self-doubt creep in, think encouraging thoughts and then make a decision to take action. Self-doubt is a road block on life's journey. The problem is not the problem, the difficulty, or the challenge, but how we react to it. You must affirm that you have the strength and the power to meet the challenge, solve the problem, achieve the goal, or get through the difficulty.

We can be so focused on not failing that we forget it is
success we are after.

Remember that there are benefits to failure. Firstly, lessons are learned from failure that will ultimately help you succeed. Secondly, by failing at something we realize it was not the way to go, and this will oftentimes send us in a different direction. This new direction consequently turns out to be for the better. Sometimes it takes failure to move you in a new and more beneficial direction.

Everything happens for a reason. Life is a journey with twists and turns, detours, and dead ends along the way, that ultimately lead us down certain roads, which lead to other roads. If you fail at something, it is for a reason. Perhaps it was not for your greater good to go down a particular path, and by failing you didn't. Sometimes good things will happen to us to lead us in a different direction. Sometimes bad things will happen to lead us down a different path, as well.

The best success stories often begin with failure. Below are many surprising failure-turned-success stories:

- RH Macy, the founder of one of the largest department store chains in the world, had numerous failed retail businesses before the hugely successful Macy's Department Store.
- Henry Ford failed at numerous automobile businesses before inventing his assembly line mode of production, which led to the success of the Ford Motor Company.
- Billionaire Bill Gates's first business failed.
- The media mogul, Jay Z, while a rapper, couldn't get a major record label to sign him, so he co-founded his own label that would ultimately become a multi-million dollar business.
- One of the greatest basketball players of all time, Michael Jordan, initially didn't make the cut on his high school varsity basketball team.
- Several of Walt Disney's businesses and movies failed before he became a media mogul.
- Sir James Dyson had many failed prototypes before his Dyson Dual Cyclone bag-free vacuum cleaner became the best selling bag-free vacuum brand in several countries.
- Stephen King's first novel was rejected by numerous publishers before it was published.
- Music legend Elvis Presley was fired after his first appearance at the Grand Ole Opry.

- A failed rice cooker was the first product of the multi-billion dollar business empire, Sony.

Even though you may fail, big time, you will succeed big time, because you will learn big time.

Mistakes are Forgivable

"Mistakes are not offences whereby men should be punished,
but rather a means by which men enrich their lives."
—Unknown

We all make mistakes. Do not be afraid of making mistakes. Like failure, mistake is a great teacher. The worst mistake you can make is to not learn from your mistakes. You have to be willing to make mistakes in order to succeed.

You can't change mistakes once they are made. However, what is most important is how you react to your mistakes. You can pay attention and learn something, or you can ignore the mistake and continue to make the same mistakes. When you are able to acknowledge the negative outcome of the mistake, you are more likely to learn from it, and avoid making it again. Alternatively, you could view the negative outcome as a threat, and consequently ignore the mistake in order to avoid feeling bad.

I have a friend who habitually dated married men when she was younger. The relationships would always end in disaster. She would always get attached, fall in love, and ultimately get hurt. Nevertheless, she repeated this same mistake over and over. Firstly, she was apparently in denial, as she failed to admit that dating a married man was a mistake. Secondly, she was afraid to admit this because admitting it would make her feel bad. If she admitted it was a mistake, she would have to admit it was a personality flaw, that it was detrimental to her emotionally, and that it was dumb. When she finally owned up to it, she stopped dating married men. As a result she was happier and guilt free.

I dated a married man once and once was enough. I would feel bad all the time, because I knew it was wrong. I never had trouble getting a single man, but somehow I got attached to this married man. Several times I broke up with him and then got back with him. Even getting my feelings hurt a few times did not make me stop. I stopped seeing him when I found out that his wife knew we were having an affair, and I realized that I had hurt her. I felt extremely guilty for a long time. For years I wanted to call her and tell her I was sorry. I just made it a point to never, ever date a married man again.

Another problem that arises with mistakes is when we don't own up to them. Our mistakes shape who we are. By admitting them, we learn from them. When you make a mistake, especially one that affects others, take responsibility. Don't make excuses. Instead of coming up with a reason to justify the mistake, own it.

Valuable wisdom is born out of mistakes, wisdom that is essential for our growth. Admitting you made a mistake is a positive response to making a mistake. Conversely, making excuses is a negative response and will have a negative effect. Let go of the need to be right. Denying you made a mistake represents defensiveness. Blaming others is a form of denial.

Mistakes are forgettable and forgivable if you own up to them.

"Wise men learn from their mistakes, but wiser men learn from the mistakes of others." —Unknown

You shouldn't have to go down every path to find out it's the wrong path. You must pay close attention to others' mistakes, not for the purpose of judging them or looking down on them, but to apply the lesson to your own benefit. If you don't apply the lessons from others' mistakes, you run the risk of ending up in the same boat. You also are never too old to learn from others' mistakes: your parents, your children, your friends, and your co-workers. Many people observe others making horrendous mistakes, yet they go down the very same road and suffer the very same consequences. These individuals don't generally learn from others' mistakes, because they think they are somehow different and the same thing won't happen to them.

I had a friend in the 1980s who was a very smart entrepreneur. He had not been a very good student when he was in college, but he was very gifted. He was a super salesman and could sell anything to anyone. He ran a very lucrative business and made a lot of money. Drugs have always been a problem in our society, and the eighties were no different. My friend would always lecture young men on the delinquency of taking drugs. He warned them not to underestimate the power of drugs and cautioned against debasing themselves with the use of drugs. I had not been in touch with this friend for a few years. When I did encounter him, I was dumbfounded. This man had started using cocaine and subsequently crack cocaine. Clearly the drugs had vitiated him, and he was no longer the man I had known. He had become what I refer to as a street urchin, one who lives and survives solely in the streets. Seeing him like that was gut-wrenching. I had a talk with him and asked him what had happened to the man who had abhorred drugs so much. He said he was so arrogant that he thought he was above getting hooked. He had thought others who took drugs got addicted because they were weak. Since he thought he was such a strong man, he felt that the same fate would not happen to him. He said: "I was a fool". This is clearly an example of an individual who failed to learn from others' mistakes.

I have heard people brag that they are perfectionists. However, this is not really a good thing. Perfectionism is actually a defense mechanism that some people use to hide their flaws, because they don't feel good about themselves.

Mistakes are normal; perfection is abnormal.

How to benefit from your mistakes:

1. You can only learn from a mistake after you admit you've made a mistake.
2. Own up to your mistake. Blaming others will prevent you from learning from your mistakes.

3. Don't give up when you make a mistake. Don't let negative emotions such as guilt stop you or cause you to abandon your dreams.
4. Be open-minded when others make mistakes, and learn from their mistakes.
5. Have the courage to make positive changes based on what you could do differently to avoid repeating the same mistake.

Fight Negative Thoughts and Feelings

Fight negative thoughts and feelings like doubt, fear, resentment, and hatred. If you let negative feelings affect you, you will suffer. Moreover, since we are all connected and are all part of the infinite mind (God), your negative thoughts and feelings about someone else will ultimately harm only you.

If you turn your attention to positive thoughts, you won't suffer. Chronic negative feelings can result in hopelessness and despair and oftentimes even worse conditions.

The following are chronic negative feelings:

- Powerlessness: Feeling that your life is out of control and there is nothing you can do about it.
- Despair: If you have a life-threatening illness and presume your life is over, you feel despair.
- Oppression: The feeling of being heavily burdened, mentally or physically by trouble or adverse conditions.
- Forsakenness: Feelings of abandonment in times of trouble.
- Alienation: Closing yourself off from others to avoid rejection and pain.
- Helplessness: Feeling unsafe and that you cannot protect yourself.
- Captivity: Feeling imprisoned or confined, which may be mental or physical.
- Uninspired: Feeling unmotivated and stuck.
- Deficiency: Feelings that you just aren't good enough and you don't measure up to others.

Negative thoughts and feelings do not solve problems, nor do negative responses to problems. Only positive responses to problems solve problems. You have the resources within you to rise above any negative thoughts. It's not enough to push negative thoughts out of your mind. To be effective, you must also focus on positive thoughts such as success and prosperity instead of poverty and lack. Remember, what you choose to focus on is what you attract to you. If you think lack, you get lack; think riches, get riches. Think success, get success. Make it a practice to make your last thoughts before falling asleep positive thoughts. This is because the law of attraction is still working while you are asleep.

Change Negative Conditions

Everyone has within them the power to change the conditions in their lives. By understanding and applying the laws of attraction and cause and effect you can change the energies in your life and consequently affect positive change in your life.

The more you focus on negative conditions in your life, the worse the negative conditions will become. Positive thoughts are more powerful than negative thoughts. Therefore, focus on what you want in your life, not on what you don't want. To have more than enough, you must eliminate all thought of limitation. To attract money, you must focus on wealth. To have what you want, you must think, feel, believe in, and see that which you desire in your life.

Many people grow up in challenging, negative, and sometimes hostile environments. They typically survive emotionally by first facing the negative condition, then devising a plan to change it. After you have made the choice to change the negative conditions or circumstances, use the power within you to make the changes. You can attract whatever it is you need in order to move towards a goal, a dream, a positive condition, a better lifestyle, and a better life. You have an abundance of resources available within you to meet your needs, whatever they may be. You can tap into your higher source of wisdom, intuitive knowledge, intelligence, and creativity. Use the tools of affirmation, creative visualization, and meditation to achieve these goals. Creative visualization is very effective in dealing with negative conditions or circumstances. Hold a challenge or problem in your mind. Then use your imagination to overcome or release negative thoughts by imagining the positive condition or circumstance. Clearly see, feel, taste, and touch the desired state. Imagine the circumstances are real in advance of them becoming so.

Do not look outside yourself to any person, or to any thing, and realize that whatever power you need you already have: It is within you.

If you are in trouble, don't focus on the trouble. Focus on a positive outcome. This means if you focus on a positive outcome, you can literally think yourself out of trouble. You're in essence focusing your energies so that they align with the energies of the universe. This may make the difference between ruin and survival. Many years ago a boyfriend of mine told me about a rule to apply if I were ever in trouble. I have no idea where the rule originated. He said, "If you're ever in trouble, pretend that you have only ten seconds to live. Use the first nine seconds to think of a plan, and use the last second to carry out your plan." This sounded like a good plan to me. This rule can be applied to many situations in life, not just life threatening situations. This rule has saved me more than a few times.

Get Rid of Dead Wood and Dead Weight

Deadwood is anything extraneous, anything that you don't need or tends to keep you in the past. It can be mental, emotional, or physical. Deadwood has the effect of holding you back.

I believe how a person's physical environment looks is reflective of their emotional and mental state. For instance, a cluttered home makes for a cluttered mind. Clutter can block your vision and mental clarity. The most significant problem with clutter, like deadwood, is that it keeps us tied to the past.

People that hold on to everything, even when they don't need it, typically possess an impoverished mentality. Clearing out the deadwood is a good way to free yourself from that state of mind. If you want something new to come into your life, make room for it. This means getting rid of personal items that you no longer need or use. When you give away items you no longer need or use, this can potentially bring about financial gain. Moreover, when you clear out deadwood, it is easier to make positive changes in your life. The more clutter in your environment, the more overwhelmed you will be. Clearing out deadwood also helps you be more creative. Therefore, constantly clean up clutter and finish projects.

> "Life is like an elevator: On your way up, sometimes you have to stop and let some people off." —Unknown

Sometimes you may have to get rid of people in your life that are dead weight. Dead weight is an oppressive burden or a person who is worthless to the greater good. Someone who physically abuses you is clearly deadweight. Negative people, people who put you down, may have a negative effect on your self-esteem. There are situations of emotional abuse that can affect self esteem, or result in depression, anxiety, and sometimes suicide. Emotional abuse includes name calling or insults, humiliation, ignoring, yelling, swearing, isolation, intimidation, constant criticism, degradation, or constant putting another down. People that are mentally, verbally, or physically abusive are dead weight. Get rid of them!

What about that person who is just plain negative? That person who constantly complains? That person who never has anything positive to say? That person that you constantly have to prop up? I refer to these people as "Debbie Downers." Then, there is that person whom your parents would call a bad influence. Bad influencers are people who are aimless, who have no goals, aspirations, or dreams. People who just exist, for no apparent purpose. There are many instances where a "good kid," who was a good student, who didn't drink or smoke, turned into someone else, seemingly overnight. This kid did not just wake up one morning and say, "I think I'll get high today, skip school, and rob someone." Somewhere along the way, this kid came into contact with a bad influence.

Bad influences are not always apparent. Even as an adult, you can have bad influences. For example, you date a guy who outside of going to work does nothing but smoke marijuana and drink. You two spend a lot of time together. Time together is spent not talking about the future, not pursuing dreams, not encouraging each other to grow, not learning, and not planning. On the contrary, time is spent drinking, getting high, having sex, and eating. Even after he's gone, you still spend your spare time getting high, drinking, eating, and getting fat.

It is not always the case that bad influences have an effect on everyone they come into contact with. For example, there was a kid who grew up around drug addicts and other kids who skipped school, got high, and engaged in criminal activity. As a matter of fact, his entire environment was negative. Somehow he came into contact with positive influences, and he decided he did not want to be like the majority of people around him. So, against the odds, he finished high school, graduated from college, and obtained two master's degrees. For a relative of his, things didn't turn out so well. He too had decided to pull away from the negative influences in his life and go to college. He agreed to let his childhood friends drive him to college, which was several hundred miles away. On the way to drop him off, the friends decided to rob a convenience store. The owner of the store resisted and ended up being fatally shot. Long story short, this relative never made it to college. Instead, he is serving a life sentence in prison.

I have always been driven and goal-oriented. If someone came into my life that was a potential bad influence, I would take flight. For instance, I once went on a cruise with a boyfriend. During the cruise, he tried to introduce me to cocaine. Once the cruise was over, so were we.

> "He that walketh with wise *men* shall be wise: but a companion of fools shall be destroyed."—Proverbs 13:20

When you associate with positive and successful people, your standards become higher. Conversely, when you associate with losers, your standards become lower. Stop bottom-feeding. Instead, seek out people who have similar positive attributes. People that are driven, goal-oriented, responsible people who have something going for them. Being around losers may also cause you to lose perspective. Compared to losers, you look like a superstar.

If you are in the habit of surrounding yourself with less ambitious people, where you are always the biggest fish in the pond, you may need to take a closer look at yourself. This need to be the biggest fish in the pond may be indicative of low self-esteem. It may also mean that you feel intimidated by people you perceive as more successful than you.

I have a relative that is very beautiful, smart, and ambitious. She has a lot going for her. She has always been a go-getter. However, she consistently dates losers. I told her she was a bottom-feeder and that she doesn't feel worthy of a successful man of substance. I also told her that her bottom-feeding would eventually affect her negatively. When I told her this, I could see the light bulb come on in her head.

Some people may come into your life for a season and for a reason, for example, to make you stronger. When people no longer contribute to your life positively, it may be time to let them go. When you find yourself compromising your happiness and your future for someone else, you may have to leave them behind. Ask yourself, what or whom can I eliminate from my life because it or they hold me back from reaching my full potential, my goals, or my dreams?

Rid Yourself of Bad Habits

In 1908, *The American Journal of Psychology* defined habit as: "A habit, from the standpoint of psychology, is more or less a fixed way of thinking, willing, or feeling acquired through previous repetition of a mental experience." Smoking, drinking excessively, and taking drugs are considered bad habits. Bad habits also include having negative thoughts, not focusing, laziness, and the like. I define a bad habit as any repetitive act that has a counter-productive or non-productive effect on an individual. Habitual behavior usually goes unnoticed by persons exhibiting the habit. This is because, as a general rule, we don't analyze what we do or think. Therefore, thinking negative thoughts are not generally noticed in individuals who habitually think negative thoughts.

We generally have a need to justify our actions, particularly bad habits. We experience conflict when we hold two opposing thoughts, acts, beliefs, or opinions. This is because these opposing thoughts, acts, beliefs, and opinions are psychologically dissonant. This dissonance typically leads to mental anguish. Take for instance, someone who believes that smoking is detrimental to their health, and knows that smoking could kill them. This person will suffer mental anguish because they smoke a pack of cigarettes a day. Now, you may be thinking that logically, this person will just quit smoking, because of the mental anguish it causes. Not so. Generally, if they have tried to quit and failed, they have to find some way to reduce this mental anguish. They typically do this by deluding themselves that smoking really isn't so harmful. They may further justify the bad habit by comparing it to something else undesirable, by deluding themselves that it is the lesser of two evils. For example, "If I stop smoking I will gain a lot of weight and become obese, and obesity is worse than smoking." They try to reconcile the idea that smoking is injurious to their health with the act of smoking. This is oxymoronic. You can't reconcile the two. Hence they suffer continuous mental anguish. These individuals not only suffer mental anguish, they are killing themselves as well.

Bad habits generally emanate from a desire to express something that some individuals feel gives life satisfaction. However, bad habits ultimately tend to do the opposite of what one initially desired or sought. You can get rid of bad habits using the power of your mind. Clearly, old habits are hard to break and new habits are hard to form, because the old habits are embedded in your subconscious mind. However, new, better habits can be formed through repetition, just as the old bad habits were formed.

Take these steps toward changing bad habits:

- Acknowledge that you have a self-destructive behavior that needs to be changed;
- Take responsibility for the habit; acknowledge that you alone are to blame for the habit;
- Recognize that change is possible, that nothing is impossible;
- Make a firm decision to change;
- Make a commitment to put in the effort and sacrifices that are required;
- Use creative visualization to visualize exactly what you want to happen;
- Expect that you will overcome the habit and reject all dependency;
- Believe that you have the power within you to change and rid yourself of the bad habit;
- Reject the concept that your life depends on your body. Internalize the concept that your life depends on your thoughts;
- Use the power of suggestion to remove your resistance to the change you are seeking. Suggestion is a subtle form of hypnotism. Suggestions similar to: "I am the perfect expression of life, and as such I am immune from any bad habits. I am aware that ____________________ is a bad habit, and signifies lack and limitation in my life. I am perfect and this thing that calls itself habit is completely destroyed and the desire is gone and the

______________________ that calls itself habit no longer exists. The word that I am now speaking is absolute";

- Use repetitive affirmations continually;
- View the change as a process and take it step by step. Make incremental goals(e.g. quit smoking for ten days, then for two weeks, and so forth);
- Be persistent and persevere through doubt, fear, discouragement, pain, discomfort, and frustration;
- Designate a day of the week as your 'get back on the horse' day, so if you temporarily lapse, you'll use all your power on that day to recommit;
- Remain doggedly determined and focused. Realize that your victory is in the process as well as the goal;
- Disassociate with others that share this same bad habit, and surround yourself with positive-thinking and positive-acting people;
- Just do it. Take constructive action *now*, not tomorrow, not whenever.

Impossible Is Impossible

"After every storm the sun will smile, for every problem there is a solution, and the soul's indefeasible duty is to be of good cheer"—William R. Alger

Nothing is impossible. Everything is possible. Allow this concept to enter into your subconscious mind. When you approach challenges with a positive mindset, amazing things can happen. Moreover, the determination and emotive energy to do something actualizes your ability to do it.

There is always an answer and a solution to every problem. Tapping into the power within you is fundamental to solving problems, overcoming obstacles, and achieving goals. You must also have a strong belief in yourself, drive, and the motivation to focus and work. Drive is the burning desire or passion to accomplish a goal. This drive will give you the impetus to push through obstacles, challenges, and problems that might stand in your way.

There are inner obstacles and outer obstacles. Inner obstacles are things like lack of confidence, negative thoughts, negative feelings, and non-belief. The outer obstacles are things like lack of financing, lack of education, homelessness, and legal problems. Both types of obstacles can be overcome. For example, in order to make something possible you may need to change your thinking and work on a positive attitude. You may also need to develop or improve certain skills and talents.

God is with us and within us. Tap into the infinite knowledge, wisdom, intelligence, creativity, and power within you. Imagination is your most powerful asset. You can do all things through the power of your mind. The only obstacle to achieving something seemingly impossible is your own thought.

If you're worried, you can't think clearly. Furthermore, if you are consumed with negative feelings or thoughts it is hard to make things happen, because you can't focus. Get quiet and let the God-power within you guide you. Be driven, believe in yourself, take action, and keep your focus on the goal, and you can accomplish anything. If you think you can't do something, you can't. If you really think you can do something, you can. If you are afraid to fail, you will fail. If you're afraid something won't be good enough, it won't.

When you know who you really are and how you fit in the Universe, you will know that everything is possible. Change your thinking to "I can and I will."

Most people don't feel comfortable dealing with problems. When faced with a problem, people tend to do three things: 1) They allow fear to take over, and they do nothing and wish the problem would just go away; 2) They deflect the problem and look for someone to blame; 3) They are indecisive, and they procrastinate. In any of these cases having a problem becomes a problem. This doesn't work, because a large part of living is about solving problems. In actuality, there is a solution to every problem. If you truly believe this, you will always find a solution to your problems.

Solving problems has more to do with your reaction to the problem than anything else. Overcoming obstacles is the key to solving problems. The focus is ultimately on the obstacles, because if there were no obstacles, there would be no problem.

Problem Solving Guidelines:

1. Clearly identify the problem;
2. Define the problem. Try to define the interest of everyone involved;
3. Identify the obstacles;
4. Meditate on the problem;
5. Get others to help with the problem or get others' viewpoints;
6. Organize data: determine the facts;
7. Formulate a strategy, plan, and objectives;
8. Make a decision;
9. Identify and designate resources available to solve the problem;

10. Implement the solution;
11. Monitor the status of your solution if required. At some point you may need to re-assess your strategy;
12. Assess whether it was the best possible solution: identify the pros and cons.

Believe You Can Fly

"Come to the edge he said. They said: We are afraid. Come to the edge, he said. They came. He pushed them… and they flew" —Guillaume Apollinaire

To believe is to accept something as true. It is trust, faith, or confidence in something or someone. When you believe in yourself, you have the confidence that you can do and handle anything. Self-confidence is belief in your abilities. You become what you believe you are. You need to start believing in the person you want to be and the life you want to have. For some this is easier said than done. However, once you have made a decision to be happy, prosperous, successful, healthy, or whatever else you desire, you can have it. You can have it if you believe you can have it.

You can have what you want, if you believe, not just that you can have it, but you must also believe that you have the power within you to make it happen.

Self-confidence is learned and can be made stronger. Lack of confidence can cause you to avoid taking risks, diminish motivation to attempt undertakings, and result in failure by promoting giving up. Low self-confidence generally reveals itself through some form of negativity. On the other hand, a self-confident person is more likely to take risks. A self-confident person is also more likely to admit mistakes and learn from them. More importantly, self-confident people instill confidence in others.

As with expectations, children's belief in their abilities emulates the belief that the parents have in the child's abilities. In other words, if you let your child know that you believe in them, they are likely to have a strong belief in themselves. By the same token, overly critical parents can erode a child's self confidence.

Parents can promote self confidence in their children in the following ways:

- Start at an early age reinforcing the "I can" concept, and disavowing "I can't";
- Lead by example;
- Teach them to never give up;
- Let them know that failure at something does not make them a failure;
- Give encouragement and positive feedback;
- Watch what you say to them or about them;
- Help your child to build competencies by encouraging them to become good at something.

The best way to cultivate and retain strong self-confidence is to recognize that you have the power within you to do all things. This is where true self-confidence originates. Once you recognize this and use it, you will be unstoppable. Everyone has infinite power within. Some don't know it. Some know it and don't know how to use it. A few know it and know how to use it. Visualizing and affirming belief in your self is a step in the right direction, as our subconscious mind accepts whatever we choose to believe. When we create a strong sense of self-confidence, we will find its positive by-products in our lives. If you believe in yourself, you will succeed. Conversely, if you do not believe in yourself, you will fail. There is a saying I heard as a small child:

"Shoot for the moon. Even if you miss you'll land among the stars"— Unknown

Self-doubt is the antithesis of believing in yourself. To believe in yourself, you need to face self-doubt and deal with it like any negative feeling. Poor self-confidence makes it difficult for us to believe in ourselves. Poor self-confidence can be an effect of having failed, and being afraid to fail again. As with everything else in life, self-confidence is about mental conditioning. Believing in yourself is a process. Start the process with prayer and affirmations. You can ask God to help you believe in yourself, or you can brainwash yourself with positive affirmations. Take control of your life by making the decision that you will believe in yourself and in God.

How to promote strong self confidence:

1. Immediately get rid of self-doubting thoughts and replace them with positive affirmations. Replace "I can't" thoughts with "I can" thoughts;
2. Don't allow others to put you down or mentally abuse you;
3. Make a list of your good attributes;
4. Reflect on and list your past accomplishments;
5. View your failures as learning experiences, and write down what you have learned from them;
6. Build confidence by setting and achieving goals;
7. Ask others their opinion of you, or what they think your strengths are;
8. Affirm that you are worthwhile;
9. Recognize and verbalize that everyone makes mistakes;
10. Every day, verbalize at least one positive thing about yourself;
11. Don't allow criticism from others to infest you. Take the criticism and do something about it if necessary;
12. Do not compare yourself to others;
13. Try new things, starting with taking baby steps;
14. Leave the past in the past;
15. Recognize your shortcomings, and ask yourself what you can do to overcome them;
16. Try, try, try, and try again;
17. Soar!

Success happens when you believe in yourself; believe in God (the universe); believe you deserve success; believe you will be successful, and believe you have the power within yourself to be successful.

Fight Public Enemy Number One—Fear

"So first of all, let me assert my firm belief that the only thing we have to fear is fear itself—nameless, unreasoning, unjustified terror which paralyzes needed efforts to convert retreat into advance"—Franklin D. Roosevelt

Fear is man's greatest enemy: fear of failure, fear of poverty, fear of criticism, and even fear of the unknown. Fear is destructive, and fear will preclude you from acting when you need to. Fear also interferes with your peace of mind. Fear is a negative thought. Whenever you allow negative thoughts such as doubt to seep into your subconscious, you will feel fear.

Fear is usually imaginary. More often than not, what we are afraid of doesn't exist. I live in the country, where houses are spaced far apart. I feel very safe and comfortable in my home. Friends and family, however, have asked me whether I felt unsafe. They have also made comments that they would be afraid to live where I live because of the seclusion. Although I have a security system, and my home is physically safe, my peace and sense of security comes from within. I also know that if I am afraid, I will attract the very thing that I am afraid of to me. In fact in the ten years I have lived in my home, there have not been any break-ins or crime of any type in my area. On the other hand, when I lived in the city previously in the best, most desirable areas, I was burglarized twice.

"Take therefore no thought for the morrow: for the morrow shall take thought for the things of itself. Sufficient unto the day *is* the evil thereof." —Matthew 6:34

Worry is fear. Do not fear what is going to happen tomorrow, because each day has enough trouble of its own. Worry, like fear, is a direct consequence of the belief in shortage, limitation, and poverty. It is disbelief in prosperity, abundance, and success. You can supplant thoughts of fear with positive thoughts such as success, victory, and achievement.

"Be strong and of a good courage, fear not, nor be afraid of them: for the LORD thy God, he *it is* that doth go with thee; he will not fail thee, nor forsake thee." –Deuteronomy 31:6

Face your fears with courage and belief in yourself and in God. God will not fail you nor forsake you. Knowing this, you can survive any situation. Fear can destroy your chances of survival in a crisis situation, if you are too afraid to think or act. In a crisis situation you need to be able to think clearly. You need to be able to think yourself out of trouble. Many people allow fear to rule their behavior instead. Remember, it is the reaction to fear that matters, not the fear itself. When faced with adversity or a crisis, *think*. Think of a plan to get out of the threatening situation and then execute the plan. During any crisis, be confident and determined. Do not waiver. Fight the fear, and by all means do not entertain the thought of defeat. Be positive and focus on your goal instead.

"LET not your heart be troubled"—John 14:1

Instead of being distressed, believe in, trust, and count on God to see you through trouble. Imagine that you are in a boat that capsizes, and it's getting dark. You determine that you have to swim to shore, because if you don't you will probably perish. Once you make the decision to swim to shore, your mind must be focused on reaching the shore. Can you imagine what would happen if the whole time you were swimming, you were thinking about drowning or getting attacked by a shark? You would lose focus, lose confidence, and probably the will and the ability to make it to shore. Also, never, ever give up, and hang on until the end. You never know if the Coast Guard might show up to rescue you.

In the face of fear, be courageous and fight the real enemy – fear.

"What time I am afraid, I will trust in thee. In God I will praise his word, in God I have put my trust; I will not fear what flesh can do unto me."—Psalm 56:3–4

If you trust in God you will not be afraid. When you have confidence in and trust in God, you know that he will help you out of trouble in your time of need. You know that when you have God on your side, you do not have to be afraid of mortal man. When you are afraid, it is important to focus on a positive outcome and continually strengthen your faith and trust in God. Pray for God to protect you when you are afraid. Then put your trust in him, knowing that everything you pray for will be fulfilled.

Courage—Don't Leave Home Without It

"Watch ye, stand fast in the faith, quit you like men, be strong." —1 Corinthians 16:13

To survive the journey of life, you must have faith and be courageous and strong. Sometimes, you must have the faith, strength, and courage to make difficult decisions. Then you must have the faith, strength, and courage to follow through with your decisions. There have been times when I've had to make very difficult decisions, like the time in my early twenties I had to make a decision in the face of death.

I had gone to the store to get a birthday card. The store was within walking distance from my house. I had a single twenty-dollar bill that I used to pay for the card. The cashier had given me nineteen single-dollar bills as change, which I shoved in the front pocket of my jeans. It was almost dark, and I was walking home down a side street.

There was a well-dressed man approximately twenty feet in front of me with a pipe in his hand. He stopped and walked towards me, then asked if I had a light. Something inside me instantly told me something was wrong. I decided to turn and run away when I heard, "Stop or I'll blow your head off." I turned slightly to see if he had a gun. Yes, there was a gun pointing straight at me. By this time he was very close to me. The man then said, "Get in the bushes".

I saw myself being found the next morning raped, naked, and possibly dead. I made the decision right then, that I was not going into the bushes. I dropped down on my knees on the concrete, in front of the man, crying a prayer to God. The man shouted, "Shut up and get in the bushes!" I kept praying. He had the nose of the gun to my temple at this time. I kept praying. The answer came to me. I pulled out the nineteen singles and told the man that I had a lot more at home, along with jewelry, televisions, and so on. I told him that I lived alone, just around the corner. He reached out to take the money, and in that instant, I bolted. I was a very fast runner to begin with, and that night I ran the race of my life. It was kind of funny because I ran in a zigzag pattern. I guess I thought I could dodge a bullet that way.

I was never more afraid in my life, but I knew I had to make a decision. I knew I had to find the courage to run away. I found the courage in prayer, and I found the answer to my prayer, right there on that concrete sidewalk.

Courage is not the absence of fear, but the fortitude to react in spite of it.

To have courage does not mean that you are not afraid. To have courage means that even though you are afraid, you face the fear and react in a positive manner to it. It takes courage to do something or get through something difficult. Sometimes we are afraid to make a decision. We are afraid that the consequences of that decision will be a mistake, will hurt someone, will cause pain, or will cause us suffering. You have to be able to do what you have to do without being afraid of the outcome. You have to face the dragons. Even if it means you might lose money, lose your freedom, not be popular, end up alone, or even die.

Make a decision: Face the dragons.

Courage Is:

- Not giving up, no matter how many obstacles stand in your way;
- Doing the thing you think you cannot do;
- Having the strength to withstand danger, fear, or difficulty;
- Taking risks;
- Fighting for your life, even though you are scared to death;
- Starting something without any guarantee that it will succeed;
- Acknowledging that you may lose, but playing anyway;
- Making something happen in the face of uncertainty;
- Having the integrity to say yes, when everyone else says no;

- Standing for what you believe in, even if that means standing alone;
- Not letting fear derail your dreams;
- Transcending your fears.

The bottom line is: courage is doing what you're afraid to do. Sometimes it is not doing something. It is also having the fortitude to face challenges and get through a tough situation or a tough time without giving up or deflecting. Anyone can be courageous. The courage to do something or not do something comes from reacting to fear in a positive way. Courage can be inspired and the capacity to act in the face of fear can be developed. The more you practice it, the greater your capacity to be courageous.

I have a brother who seems not to be afraid of anything. This is probably because he has greatly developed his fortitude to face fear. This development of courage likely started when he was about eight years old. There was a bully that would harass him at school and even follow him home. My brother was so afraid of him he oftentimes would run straight home from school and lock himself in the house. One day, my dad happened to be at home when my brother ran into the house, clearly frightened. My dad asked, "Boy, what is wrong with you?" Hesitantly, my brother responded that this really bad boy was going to beat him up and had chased him home. The bully had the audacity to be standing outside our house challenging my brother to come out. My Dad said, "Oh, h--- no! You are going to go back out there and stand up to that boy." In tears, my brother replied, "He's bigger and stronger than me, and he's very mean." My father then directed him to go outside and deal with the bully or face the consequences with him. As my brother wanted no part of my dad, he walked toward the door, trembling and crying. My Dad instructed him to stop crying and not to show fear. He explained how standing up to the bully would make him leave my brother alone. He also underscored the point that my brother would be more afraid of him if he didn't go out there and face the bully.

Long story short, my brother fought and beat the bully, although he took a pretty good beating himself. The bully never bothered him again. As it turned out, the bully was not very much larger or stronger than my brother. However, the bully's threatening attitude, actions, and demeanor is what really frightened my brother. In actuality, there was really nothing to fear but fear itself.

The greater the fear, the greater the courage required to overcome it.

Courage generally emanates from attributes like faith or determination. To have courage, you must have the confidence to trust yourself and to trust in God for the right direction, and you must rely on the power within you.

Defeat, Defeat

Life can sometimes wear you out. Thus, you feel defeated and lose confidence. This can lead to complacency and mediocrity. There are many people who have overcome great challenges and obstacles. You must believe that you can overcome all obstacles as well. You have the potential to triumph over whatever negative ideas, conditions, or circumstances confront you. Therefore, when you encounter obstacles (which you will), make up your mind to jump over them, run through them, or go around them.

When you get discouraged, you are most vulnerable to defeat. Negative feelings like discouragement and fear will take away your power. At these times you must shift from negative- to positive-thinking, as most obstacles are mental. You can supplant defeatist thoughts with thoughts of confidence, success, achievement, and power. To avoid a defeatist attitude, keep in mind that the universe (God) is with you and helping you. Therefore, stay the course.

It's not over when you're defeated; it's over when you quit.

Turn lemons into lemonade. This axiom, which I have practiced all my life, refers to turning problems into opportunities, benefitting or profiting from your mistakes and failures, or making something good out of a bad situation. Rather than feeling defeated, think of success and turn any negative situation around. In order to turn lemons into lemonade, you must learn to systematically see the good in the bad. You do this by changing your point of view and reacting positively instead of negatively to bad situations. For example, when bad things occur, most people respond with negative feelings of anger, frustration, and hurt. Instead they should remain calm and think of how to turn the situation around. Always be aware that a positive response will typically create something productive.

Ways to implement the lemons-to-lemonade principle:

1. When you encounter a problem, stop any negative thoughts from getting into your mind. This is necessary before you can allow positive, productive thoughts in.
2. Once you have negative feelings under control, brainstorm positive alternatives, opportunities, or outcomes. You must be in a calm, relaxed state for this to be productive.
3. Assess the brainstorming possibilities and determine a course of action, then implement the course of action.

The following is a good example of turning lemons into lemonade. A friend's husband told her out of the blue that he wanted a divorce and was going to move out of their home in thirty days. My friend was devastated. She didn't see it coming. Instead of getting upset, depressed, or angry, she remained calm. She asked him if he was absolutely sure that was what he wanted. When he answered yes, she knew she had a problem to deal with, as she did not make enough income on her own to pay all of her household bills. Rather than freak out, she asked God for guidance, then started brainstorming ways to make ends meet. As a result of her brainstorming, she came up with the idea to provide room and board to an elderly person. To make a long story short, the income from the one elderly client was enough to pay all her bills. She ultimately took in two more clients, and was able to quit her job and start a profitable business.

Think defeated, be defeated.

Think you're a winner, be a winner.

Have it Your Way—Expect Success

"Ask, and it shall be given you;
Seek, and ye shall find;
knock, and `it shall be opened
unto you:
For every one that asketh
receiveth;
and he that seeketh
findeth;
and to him that knocketh
It shall be opened." —Matthew 7:7–8

We don't always get what we want or need. We usually, however, will not get more than we expect. The thing you expect to happen usually comes to pass, whether it's positive or negative. Stop expecting failure. If you expect failure, you will fail. When things are tough, expect them to get better. When business is bad, expect it to turn around. Once you expect success, how to succeed falls into place.

Always expect something good to happen, no matter what happened yesterday.

This principle of expectation is a subtle underpinning of the law of attraction. In addition to using thought to create that which you wish to manifest, you must expect the desired results. Furthermore, the greater the expectation, the more likely the desired result will manifest. This principle is what the placebo effect is based on. The placebo effect is the effect when a fake drug is given to a patient (or test subject), and the patient's body reacts favorably to it, as though it were a real drug. The widely accepted theory is that the placebo effect is due to an individual's expectations. Medical professionals also assert that there is a correlation between how strongly a person expects to have results and whether or not the expected results will occur.

We should expect success to be successful. But what is success? Each person's definition of success is different, but it always comes down to winning and achievement. It is essentially getting what you desire. Success can be attained with anything, whether business, personal, or financial.

Sometimes people accomplish what others expect them to accomplish. This sometimes accounts for why so many seemingly intelligent people don't succeed. Many are influenced by people around them, who systematically destroy their self-confidence. Regardless of others' expectations of you, you can choose success. You have the power to choose positive thoughts and expect positive results, which will manifest success. Your subconscious mind will manifest what you expect.

Self-fulfilling prophecy is the theory that a false prophecy, whether positive or negative, whether a strongly-held belief or a delusion, when declared to be true, may sufficiently influence the believer so that their reactions ultimately fulfill the once-false prophecy. In other words, people react to what they perceive a situation to be (even if the perception is false). Essentially, their reaction to this perception actually brings about the perceived state.

An example of self-fulfilling prophecy from Greek mythology is the story of Oedipus. Believing that one day his newborn child Oedipus would kill him, Laius left him alone to die. Oedipus was, however, found and raised by foster parents. When he grew up, he was told he would kill his father and marry his mother. Oedipus left home and went to Greece, unaware that his foster parents were not his biological parents. While in Greece, he got into a fight with a stranger and killed him, unaware that this stranger was his biological father. He subsequently married the stranger's widow, who was actually his biological mother.

This theory also asserts that one's expectations about another person eventually leads the other person to behave in ways that substantiate these expectations. For instance, studies have shown that where high expectations were made known to students, they performed positively. Conversely, where low expectations were made known to students they performed accordingly. Always expect the best of others, especially children, as your attitude towards them will come back to you. For example, if you think your child is bad, and you expect him to be bad, he will pick up that expectation from you and his behavior will be bad. The same holds true of employees. If an employee believes that you think he is incompetent, he will be incompetent.

If you truly expect something, you will take action in preparation of that expectation. If you were expecting a baby, wouldn't you start accumulating those things necessary to bring the baby home? If you expect to go to college and become a doctor, wouldn't you take the proper preparatory courses? This is true of expectations of success. Successful people expect their actions to produce success, so they take steps to make it happen. However, your actions must be aligned with your expectations. This is a common problem with new business people. If you expect your lawn service to be successful, why are you detailing cars and doing everything but preparing your lawn service for success? This scenario sounds like someone who doesn't expect his business to be successful, so he is hedging.

The fear of failure or the fear of success may derail your expectancy of success. Fear of success sounds counterintuitive. It is actually a subconscious reaction to the possibility of success, which may manifest in various ways. It may manifest in self-sabotage, which includes loss of focus, not focusing to begin with, procrastination, second-guessing yourself, and making excuses. Other symptoms include being easily distracted, doubting if your work is good enough, and jumping from one project or goal to another. Generally, the closer you get to success, the higher the probability you will become frightened. The excitement of success feels uncomfortable, and nervousness ensues. You become afraid that something is going to go wrong. You have doubts that lead to lack of confidence, anxiety, and fear. Fear is always counter-productive. It causes you to focus on the perceived threats instead of crossing the finish line.

Moreover, the idea of change is uncomfortable and you worry prematurely that the success can't be sustained, that you will be out of your comfort zone, and about new pressures and responsibilities that come with success. You must confront these thoughts and feelings. Ask yourself, "What is the worst that can happen when I become successful? What is the best that can happen when I become successful?" You also might be a victim of not believing in yourself. Reinforce your belief in yourself and don't give up. You can practice affirmations such as: "I am successful and I believe in myself and my abilities".

Probably, the most critical aspect of the fear of success is thinking that you don't deserve success. Feeling undeserving will prevent you from attaining success. In order to truly expect success, you must feel that you deserve success. If you feel undeserving, you will find a way to sabotage your impending success. Your sense of self as undeserving will drive you to self-sabotage. You must confront and challenge your undeserving thoughts and feelings. Oftentimes it is low self-esteem and negative experiences in your past that cause you to feel undeserving. Underpinning low self-esteem and negative experiences are negative feelings like shame, guilt, and emotional trauma. These thoughts and feelings must be reconciled. You must firstly attempt to understand the origins of these thoughts and feelings. Secondly, you must forgive yourself and forget the past negative experiences. Ask yourself, "Why should everyone who has achieved success deserve it and not me? Why do I think or feel that I don't deserve this success?"

How does one go about attaining success?

Guide to attaining success (based on my own experiences and experiences of others):

- Concentration: Concentrate all of your resources and your energies toward the attainment of your objectives, goals, or dreams. Take a rifle approach, rather than a shotgun approach. If you spread yourself too thin, it will take you longer to attain success, or it may not happen at all. Focus on the prize, and keep your eye on the prize. Therefore, don't start two businesses at the same time. Don't try to quit smoking and drinking at the same time. Don't try to be a director and an actor at the same time. Of course there are exceptions to the rule, but generally diluting your resources and energies doesn't work. Andrew Carnegie forewarned: "Put all of your eggs into one basket and then watch your basket."

- Your Focus: Do not make the attainment of wealth your goal. Focus on doing what you do well and on serving others, and the wealth will follow.
- Make Goals: Formulate and write down your goals and your plan for success.
- Preparation: Piss-poor preparation makes for piss-poor results. The seven Ps are thought to have originated as a British army axiom. Although widely purported in business, it is applicable to many circumstances in life in general.
- Take responsibility: As only you are responsible for you, only you are responsible for your own success. Don't ever blame others and don't make excuses. Your success or failure is on you and no one else: not your mother, not your father, not your wife. No one else.
- Learn: Learn as much about the area of your desire as you possibly can. This may mean taking classes, doing research, or asking for advice. If your goal is to successfully quit smoking, do the research and find out what the best method is for you. Find out everything about addictions, everything about breaking bad habits, everything about medicines that help you quit. Become the expert on quitting smoking (or whatever it is you're aiming to be a success at).
- Network: Associate with and network with like-minded, progressive people.
- Help Others: Don't just look for help from others. When you help others the universe (God) will help you.
- Don't Retreat: Don't let anything or anyone come between you and your goals and dreams.
- Shoot for the Moon: Aim high and strive to be the very best. Go over and above what's expected of you. Don't let others limit your potential.
- Persist: Don't ever, ever, give up.
- Fight fear: Learn to recognize and fight both types of fear: fear of failure and fear of success.

Dreams do come true. Miracles do happen—only if you expect them to.

Be inspired

"Life is like riding a bicycle. To keep your balance, you must keep moving."—Albert Einstein

Getting in touch with and living in alignment with what touches our heart and soul inspires us. This results in good emotions like excitement, joy, and happiness. Hence, when you feel good, you become driven. You become consumed by the desire to succeed and to reach the goal you wish to attain. You must determine what inspires you and get in touch with your innermost aspirations.

We have a tendency to look outside ourselves for inspiration when in fact we should be looking within ourselves. Internal inspiration is a formidable force. Inspiration is the primary source of energy that propels us to take action, and this energy comes from within. When we look outward to others who seemingly are successful and fulfilled, we oftentimes become frustrated by our own realities. Inspiration is generally motivated by extreme desire, however, it can be driven by fear.

Self-actualization is self-inspiring, as self-actualized people tend to be inspired. Reassess what gives you the greatest possible satisfaction. We have within ourselves a source of personal satisfaction. Recognize what success is for you. Determine what drives you and what makes you passionate. When you are doing something that makes you feel good, excited, and like you can't wait to do it, then you are inspired.

What matters most to you?

What is it you really want out of life?

What are your priorities?

Once you have made these determinations, your willingness and emotive energy for success will lead to the ability to succeed. When you are clear and enthusiastic about what you want, and you are willing to do what it takes to get it, you will succeed. When you are inspired you achieve success.

If you don't chase your dreams, you will never catch them.

We are also inspired or not inspired by what we believe. If you believe that the cards are stacked against you and you don't believe in yourself, then you're likely not to be inspired. On the other hand, if you believe in the power of your subconscious mind and believe that you can do and be anything, this will inspire you.

25 Tips on how to inspire yourself:

- Have concrete goal(s) to shoot for and write them down.
- Gain confidence from reading and learning about your goal.
- Deal with any mental blocks such as excuses, doubts, and fears: think them through, then squash them.
- Break your goal down into realistic segments.
- Turn your goal(s) into an adventure. Make it more about the journey.
- Think about the exciting opportunities that lie ahead when you achieve your goal(s).
- Plan and manage your time, and develop a routine.
- Believe in yourself and trust yourself.
- Avoid negative thoughts, such as fear.
- Read others' success stories.
- Team up with a co-motivator.
- Brainstorm with others.
- Constantly read inspirational books and articles.
- Surround yourself with optimistic people.
- Listen to upbeat music and music with positive inspirational messages.

- Commune with nature.
- Prioritize and focus on what you want.
- Establish rewards for passing milestones and achieving your ultimate goal.
- Be grateful for what you have and stay hopeful for what you want.
- Use creative visualization regularly.
- Use positive affirmations regularly.
- Use inspirational quotes to help inspire you and keep you inspired.
- Get rid of distractions.
- Remove some things off your plate if it is full.
- Keep yourself excited about your goal.

You Snooze You Lose—
Stop Procrastinating

"Even so faith, if it hath not works, is dead, being alone. Yea, a man may say, Thou hast faith, and I have works: shew me thy faith without thy works, and I will shew thee my faith by my works."—James 2:17–18

Faith by itself is not enough. Without action to back it up, faith is inoperative. Sometimes we may need to take some type of action in order to promote our thoughts, wants, and dreams. In other words, you may have to put yourself in a position to receive what you want. So move from thinking, imagining, and feeling to action.

Success is not based on what you are going to do, but what you actually do.

Law of attraction + action = success.

Sometimes getting what you want is a one-step process, which entails merely thinking the thing into existence. Sometimes it may require just one act on your part, or it may take multiple actions. For instance, as you take action, you attract something that you need to move to the next level, then you take action again and you attract what you need, and so forth. The more affirmative action you take, the more you move toward what you want.

"Don't wait for your ship to come in, *swim out to it*."
—Unknown

Procrastination is intentionally putting off something that should be done. Procrastination is counterproductive. It can result in negative outcomes and emotions such as stress, anxiety, and guilt. This stress, anxiety, and guilt can cause one to procrastinate even more. The causes of procrastination continue to be debated amongst psychologists. Some believe there is a nexus between anxiety, low self-esteem, low self-confidence, learned helplessness, and a self-defeating mentality. Chronic procrastination has been connected to depression as well. It is also associated with people who have a tendency to negatively evaluate outcomes. Procrastination may also be a coping mechanism for the anxiety associated with starting or completing a task or making a decision. Telling yourself that you work better under pressure at the last minute, using activities like surfing the Internet or watching TV to avert attention from the procrastinated task, and telling yourself that you are not procrastinating but taking care of more important tasks, are all justifications and excuses.

"Knowing is not enough; we must apply. Willing is not enough; we must do."—Johann Wolfgang von Goethe

Procrastination may be hindering your success, as it is a way of self-sabotage. It is also a self-control problem. For every reason or excuse you have not to move towards your dreams, there is probably an act to overcome the excuse or reason. Change your thought or idea into an action plan. Then follow through with action to make your dreams materialize. Start with creating an overview of your dream to see the full picture, then plan the details needed to achieve your dream.

"The secret of getting ahead is getting started"—Mark Twain

How to "Just do It":

1. Make a firm decision to start;
2. Pick a start date;
3. Be clear on where and how to start;

4. Take one step at a time;
5. Focus. Concentrate your resources, your time, and your power;
6. Remind yourself why you should do what you need to do;
7. Make sure your actions are in sync with your thinking;
8. Make a deal with yourself or promise yourself a reward for finishing your goal;
9. Give yourself pep talks;
10. Start with small steps;
11. Start early in the day;
12. Start with the most difficult job first;
13. Work from a to-do list;
14. Set aside time to work;
15. Think about your successes and not your failures when commencing a goal;
16. Think of your tasks as adventures;
17. Be optimistic;
18. Stay on track. Designate a day of the week to re-motivate yourself and re-affirm your goal(s);
19. Cut down or eliminate the time you spend on social media and watching TV;
20. Post visible motivational quotes;
21. Use the fear of what will happen (or not happen) if you don't take action;
22. Focus on a positive outcome;
23. Take the first step. Just start!
24. Handle your business.

Do not wait for anything; the time will never be the right time.

Keep Your Eye on the Ball

"A person who aims at nothing will surely hit it."—Unknown

To focus is to give your all to one thing. It means that you are committed and you will not let anything or anybody get in your way. It also entails seeing one thing through to the end at the cost of all other possibilities. Goals and dreams are far more attainable when you focus on them one at a time. Trying to work on multiple goals at one time will tend to de-motivate, over-burden, and overwhelm you. Multi-tasking is actually the anti-thesis of focusing.

Distraction is the number one enemy of focus. You must determine how to eliminate distractions. Sometimes I look at people who are *always* texting, on Facebook, Twitter, and other social media sites, and I wonder, "How in the world can they possibly focus on important things?" Important things like school, work, business, and achieving their dreams and goals? The answer is: they don't focus, and they don't achieve.

Lack of self-discipline is the number two enemy of focus. Discipline is self-control, the assertion of willpower over more base desires. Self-discipline is to some degree a substitute for motivation. It is the ability to control one's feelings and conquer one's weaknesses. It entails the capability to pursue one's goals despite temptations to abandon them. A disciplined person is one who has established a goal and is willing to achieve that goal above all else. For instance, most people work hard when they feel motivated. A self-disciplined person is able to still work hard and focus even when they're not feeling motivated.

Note to self: stay focused.

You might also lose focus because you or someone else has talked you out of pursuing your dreams. When you start to doubt, you start to lose focus. When you are unable to focus and follow through, it generally means that you don't really, really believe in what you are doing. You're thinking, "Maybe I'd better hedge and go over there and work on that other thing in case the thing I'm working on doesn't work out." In this case, you are focusing on failure and not success.

People who jump from one project or business to another, without completing the previous project, have usually let negative feelings like doubt and fear stop them. These people tend to fail because of their failure to focus and follow through. These people who chronically fail to follow through, who start projects but never finish, who move from project to project, are like gerbils running around aimlessly on their little wheels.

"If you chase two rabbits, *both* will escape."—Unknown

If you find yourself running around aimlessly, narrow your focus to change the game. The real power in winning comes when you narrow your focus. Concentrate your resources and energy to achieve results. Pick one thing at a time to focus on. One business, one idea, one project, and then eat, drink, and sleep that one thing.

Success is about the capacity to focus and concentrate.

Successful people realize that there is a process involved in getting to their goals and dreams, and they focus on the process. They realize the results will take care of themselves. Successful people are in love with the process of achieving their goals and dreams. Sometimes the difference between winners and losers is being committed to the process. For example, an author who wants a bestselling book focuses on the process of writing the book. I am in love with writing. I can't wait to sit down and write, therefore I focus on writing. A basketball team in the playoffs cannot focus on the end result of the game, but must focus on the process of playing the game well. The winning of the game will happen. If the team (or individual player) is thinking, "What if we don't win?" this negative thought will affect their ability to win. To succeed you must give that something your full attention. Furthermore, if you can't focus, you can't be optimally productive. Focus is critical to getting you the results you want.

Focus on the journey, not the destination.

Focus, focus, focus! Do not let anything or anyone distract you. Keep your eye on the ball. It is not easy to keep your eye on the ball, as you may encounter many opportunities on the way, which will distract you. Disregard these distractions of less fruitful pursuits. You must constantly remind yourself of where you are going. Remind yourself that there is a reason why basketball teams only play with one ball at a time.

Tips on how to stay focused:

- Write down your goals and objectives. Be clear on what your goal is or where you are going;
- Use a focus mantra or affirmations to stay focused (use them daily or when you feel that you're getting distracted). For example, "I keep my eye on the ball";
- Control your thoughts and nip negative self-talk in the bud, as staying positive helps you focus;
- Use creative visualization to help you focus;
- Prioritize your goals, objectives, and actions;
- Minimize distractions;
- Avoid people and circumstances that tempt you to veer off your path;
- Go underground. Isolation may be required;
- Do something toward achieving your goal every day;
- Schedule times to complete actions or tasks;
- Establish milestones with rewards;
- Associate and communicate with focused, driven people.

Quitting is not an Option

"And *even* to *your* old age I *am* he; and *even* to hoar hairs will I carry you: I have made, and I will bear; even I will carry, and will deliver you."—Isaiah 46:4

If you are suffering, know that God will carry you through the tough times. He will sustain you and save you. Suffering is not important. What is important is getting over the suffering in order to move forward. Suffering is temporary, and you determine how long it will last. If you have suffered pain, hurt, emotional or physical trauma, and you lived through it, this is proof that you can handle anything that comes your way. Pray for the ability to be strong while withstanding pain or hardship.

"Count the garden by the flowers, never by the leaves that fall. Count your life with smiles and not the tears that roll"—Unknown

Have you ever just wanted to give up and die? If you have it's because you're focused on the difficulties of your life. In times like these you need to get perspective. Things always look worse when you look through the eyes of hopelessness instead of the eyes of hope. Therefore, instead of focusing on your suffering, think about happier times.

"Everything will be okay in the end. If it's not okay, It's not the end"—Unknown

On this road we call life there is always something great and amazing waiting ahead. You may have to travel this road with its twists and turns, its potholes and sinkholes, its detours, and sometimes it's head-on collisions to get to the great and amazing thing. If you are traveling on a rough road that seems like it will never end, don't turn back and don't quit. Many have traveled down this same rocky road. As you may have, they have run out of gas and had to walk; they have been lost; they have hitchhiked a ways; they have climbed uphill on foot; they have even traveled in the dark. They didn't turn back or quit because they ran into obstacles. They kept going and going until they reached their destination. It's okay to sit down briefly and rest awhile, but not for too long. If you stumble and fall along the way, get right up and continue on your journey. You never know how long this rocky road will be and you never know what's just around the bend. Therefore, focus on the road ahead and keep going and endure to the end. Things will get better.

"Tough times don't last, tough people do." —Gregory Peck

Although the future may look dark and cloudy, and you may feel like giving up, never, ever give up. Things can change in your life in the blink of an eye. When the storms of life hit, brace yourself and push through. The storm will subside. The sun will shine again.

I was driving to an appointment when I passed through a torrential rain storm. It was a frightening situation because the roads were flooded, the sky was ominous, the wind was strong, and I could hardly see through my windshield. Just as I was about to pull off to the shoulder of the road the storm stopped abruptly, and it changed from storm to sunshine in a nanosecond. It was so fast it startled me. I had passed through storms before. Normally I would pass through a transitional area where it was gray and dreary but not stormy before getting to an area that was sunny. It was astonishing to see just how quickly things changed from murky darkness to immense light, from cataclysmic storm to tranquil calm, and from trepidation to a feeling of relief.

Life isn't about waiting for the storm to pass, it's about continuing on through the storm until you reach the sunshine.

I am one of those people who really dislike cold, dreary weather. During the winter months, I basically hibernate. I look forward to spring.

Just as I know spring always comes after winter, I know that calm always comes after the storm, that daylight always comes after the night. So it is with trouble in life. If you feel troubled, try seeing life as it could be, not as it is.

"When you come to the end of your rope, tie a knot and hang on"—Franklin D. Roosevelt

Stay the Course—Perseverance and Endurance

"That which does not kill us makes us stronger." —Friedrich Nietzsche

Perseverance is doggedly pursuing your goals in the face of adversity, even with disappointments and setbacks. It is falling down and getting right up to try again, over and over if necessary. Part of persevering is overcoming obstacles and challenges along the way. When you fall down, whether due to your own fault, someone else's fault, or no one's fault, it is important to pick yourself up, salvage what you can, recover, and move on. It is continually trying until you reach that goal, cross that finish line, or climb to the top of that mountain. Endurance is the strength or power to withstand pain and hardships. If you persevere and endure during difficult times, you will ultimately be blessed for it. You must learn to live through periods of darkness. You must know in your heart that the light will come.

"Losers quit when they are tired. Winners quit when they've won." —Unknown

Perseverance entails being patient. Perseverance and patience typically exist side by side. You must wait patiently while persevering. Patience is necessary to combat adversity. Through patience and perseverance, you can accomplish amazing things. Impatience can be counterproductive and derail positive outcomes. It can cause you to do ill-advised things, or make unintelligent choices. Impatience prolongs the road to success. It does not make it shorter. It can preclude you from reaching your full potential.

Do not give up your dreams if the results you are seeking do not happen exactly when you want or expect them to happen. Be patient and keep going—you'll win. Allow impatience to incite you to quit, and you'll lose.

"If you are going through hell, keep going"—Winston Churchill

Perseverance is a dynamic quality. If you tire of hardships and quit, you will lose. You never know how close you may be to success. When you persevere you ultimately get to a point where you realize that you are very close to success. This realization leads to increasingly greater inspiration and drive. In like manner, it is through drive and inspiration that we have the power to persevere. If you really believe in your heart that you will reach your goal, you will consequently have the power necessary to propel you to attain your goal.

The strength to endure a difficult life is a far greater treasure than an easy life.

When trouble comes we tend to think, "Why me?" We think we are the only one that sees trouble and heartache. We look at others and think that they have trouble-free lives. The truth is, everyone has a sad story. *Everyone.* Everyone has gone through struggle or will go through struggle. You can never know someone's struggles just by looking at them. Those who have struggled are able to endure more than those who have not, as endurance builds character. When you run into difficulties or trouble of some sort, you will live through them. The more you persevere in the face of adversities, the stronger you will become. As a consequence, you will be better able to deal with any future adversities. Therefore, in the face of trouble of any kind, remember that your primary goal is to persevere and to endure.

The longer you endure hardship, the greater the victory of overcoming the hardship.

All hardship and struggle affords us the opportunity to see what we are truly made of, and what we are capable of overcoming. Your hardships help create the person you are. Each hardship, struggle, and obstacle induces us to learn and grow. Overcoming these hardships, struggles, and obstacles causes us to extend ourselves beyond our known capabilities. Success is, above all else, about enduring struggle.

Strength comes from struggle, not from the absence of struggle.

"Fall seven times, get up eight."—Japanese proverb

When you get knocked down a few times and you get right back up, this prepares you for when you get knocked down really hard. It will give you the strength to endure the pain and get right back up again. Moreover, people who know struggle have a special sensitivity to others who struggle, and are able to help others through tough times with compassion and understanding.

True winners are those who have felt the cold sting of defeat, who have caressed their suffering, who have intimately danced with struggle, who have stared the cold face of fear down, and who have grappled with loss, yet they have pressed on.

Know When to Fold 'Em

"But I say unto you, That ye resist not evil: but whosoever shall smite thee on thy right cheek, turn to him the other also." —Matthew 5: 39

To resist means to fight, struggle against, antagonize, assault, suffer, and persist. Therefore, resistance fails because it is contrary to peace and order. To resist evil also means to always be positive about negative circumstances, to think everything is good, even things like misery, unhappiness, death, and disease. This means that you must see problems in a different light. Instead of seeing the negative, see the positive and react positively to negative people and things.

Imagine two scenarios. Your significant other comes home in a bad mood, and calls you a negative name. In scenario number one, you call him a really nasty name. What happens? The situation escalates. In scenario number two, you kiss him on the cheek and ask him if he wants anything, and later you calmly discuss your feelings. The outcome is markedly different. One result produces more negative feelings. The other produces a positive outcome.

After you acknowledge a problem, you must take *positive* action to solve the problem. This is because whenever you release positive energy, you receive positive energy back. Sometimes when you encounter a problem, obstacle, or difficulty, it is best not to struggle with it. This is not the same as giving up.

If you go through life struggling, fighting, resisting, and opposing, you will likely become so focused on fighting that you lose sight of your original objective or goal. In other words, if you use negativity to fight negativity, you don't resolve the issue. Positive thoughts will always neutralize negative thoughts and things.

Many years ago, a boyfriend of mine was having trouble with his ex-girlfriend. She was harassing him and wouldn't leave him alone. She subsequently started harassing me. This boyfriend suggested that I call her and threaten her legally if she did not leave us alone. I called her and did just that. This was absolutely the worse thing I could have done. Shortly thereafter, I was spending the night at his place. We were in bed when we heard a noise at the window. Before I knew it, this woman had come through the bedroom window and attacked me. She left a long scratch down one side of my face. I was livid and vowed to her face that I would go to the police and file battery charges against her. It didn't end there. The woman made it to the police station before me and filed a complaint against me, alleging she had come to the door and I had attacked her. We both got arrested on battery charges. The charges were subsequently dropped after we both agreed to mediation. The initial negative situation was made worse because I used negativity to solve the problem, instead of positivity, such as kindness and understanding.

> "But I say unto you, Love your enemies, bless them that curse you, do good to them that hate you, and pray for them which despitefully use you, and persecute you" —Matthew 5:44

Extending a loving thought or gesture to someone dissolves the negativism and antagonism they have towards you. Moreover, by blessing and trying to understand problems, problematic people, obstacles, trouble, and the like, you eliminate them. You neutralize trouble by implementing an opposite state of consciousness. Therefore, trouble will cease as you remove trouble from your consciousness. Use a mantra that you can repeat to yourself to remind yourself to neutralize a problem. I use the mantra (which can also be used as an affirmation):

It's all good all the time.

Being a die-hard entrepreneur, over the years I have tried many things and have owned several businesses. Approximately half of the businesses failed. I didn't take the failings personally. I simply thought that they were not the paths I was supposed to go down. Sometimes, when we persistently struggle to achieve a goal but have little to no success, this is a forewarning for us to change paths. In effect, obstacles may be blocking your way in order to inform you that your thoughts are not aligned with your desires.

Winners never quit and quitters never win. You've got to know when to hold 'em, know when to fold 'em. These may sound like contradictory messages. The truth is both are valid axioms in the proper context. Sometimes we have to cut our losses and move on, then start over again. The challenge is knowing when to relinquish one goal and move on to another. By the same token, you don't quit just because something is difficult. You've got to know when folding is tantamount to quitting and when folding is a transitional move. You've got to know when it's right to walk away, and when it's not.

Don't Worry Be Happy

"Don't worry, be happy," a simple philosophy coined by Indian sage Meher Baba, became an iconic saying in the sixties. Characterized by a smiling face, the saying became very popular, and it was seen everywhere. Inspirational posters, cards, t-shirts, cups, and so on were printed. It regained popularity in 1988 when the artist Bobby McFerrin released a song entitled, "Don't Worry Be Happy".

Happiness is a state of mind. You can decide to be happy now: not tomorrow, not when you graduate, not when you get married, not when your children leave home, not when you've solved all your problems, but now. You need only make that decision. You can't allow financial, marital, or any other problems to determine your state of happiness. You should enjoy every single day of your life, regardless of whatever challenges you may be facing. Many people fail to be happy because they focus too much on the past and the future. Focus on the now. Don't dwell on the past or worry about the future.

"Most folks are as happy as they make up their minds to be."
—Abraham Lincoln

You probably know someone who lives in a constant state of unhappiness. They are always angry, upset, frustrated, and worried. I was like that for a while. I always had a frown on my face. I was frequently getting upset over little things. My two-and-a-half-year-old grandson plays the game Angry Birds on my cell phone. One day I was very impatient with him and was fussing at him rather harshly. After I scolded him, he asked, "GiGi are you an angry bird?" I laughed and said, "Yes, I am." That is when I decided to be happy and not let anything cause me to be upset or not at peace. Once I made the decision to be happy, I made a list of the things I could do to stay happy.

Many people also make the mistake of thinking that someone else can make them happy. The truth of the matter is that if you are not happy by yourself, you certainly will not be happy with someone else. A daughter of an acquaintance of mine sleeps with a lot of men and always has to have them around. Her mom asked me to speak to her about this. After speaking with her, she said that she doesn't see this as a problem. She claims that she just likes sex. In my opinion, she is very unhappy, and she keeps looking for a man to make her happy. She will continue to be unhappy and in a constant state of searching until she decides that no one else can make her happy, and until she is happy by herself. Typically, people who cannot be alone don't like themselves. In other words they have low self-esteem. If you love yourself, you will be more inspired to pursue your own happiness. Pursue happiness from within and stop searching for happiness through others. Just be happy!

You find happiness within, not without.

Become aware of the things that make you happy. Keep a journal to help discern what specifically triggers feelings of happiness in you. Ask yourself whether you are enjoying the life you are living. If the answer is no, you must seek out the things that make you happy, pursue them, and learn to savor the moments that bring you happiness.

How to make yourself happy:

1. Make a conscious decision to be happy;
2. Be happy to be alive;
3. Make happy affirmations;
4. Have some fun;
5. Have goals to look forward to;
6. Take care of your body;
7. Stay connected to friends and family. Do not isolate yourself;
8. Keep a journal;
9. Do something creative;
10. Travel;

11. Learn something new. Take a class;
12. Have an 'I love myself' day;
13. Have a 'do nothing' day;
14. Have a 'staycation';
15. Renovate or rearrange your home;
16. Give a party;
17. Pretend you are a visitor to your own city or state and be adventurous;
18. Give yourself treats and rewards;
19. Smile more;
20. Laugh more;
21. Strive to achieve self-actualization.

Self-Actualization

The concept of self-actualization gained prominence with Abraham Maslow's theory of the hierarchy of needs. Maslow recognized self-actualization as the highest level of psychological development that can be achieved. Theoretically, when one reaches this level, their full personal potential has been fulfilled. Moreover, people are motivated to fulfill basic needs before moving on to other, more advanced needs. Maslow's theory mandates that if you don't meet the lower level needs first, you will have a very difficult—if not impossible—time attaining the highest level of self-actualization.

Viewed as a pyramid, the lowest levels represent the most basic needs, and the higher up you go the more complex the needs are. Needs at the bottom are comprised of basic physical needs, including the need for food, water, sleep, and warmth. Once these lower level needs are met, you're able to move up to the next level of needs, which are for safety and security, and so on. As you progress up the hierarchy, your needs become more psychological and social. It has been found that fulfillment of these needs is strongly related to happiness.

Initially there were five levels. In subsequent writings, this number was expanded to eight. The eight levels are:

1. Physiological Needs: Survival needs, such as the need for food, water, air, sleep, and excretion. Also included is the need for sex, stability, and freedom from fear.
2. Safety and Security Needs: These include the need for steady employment or income, shelter from adverse weather conditions, safe environments, and access to health care.

3. Social Needs: The need for love and affection, a sense of belonging, sexual intimacy. Marriage, friendships, family, and other social groups satisfy this need.
4. Self-Esteem: The need for personal worth, recognition, status, prominence, prestige, accomplishment, self-respect, and respect from others. This also includes the need for the things that reflect high self-esteem.
5. Cognitive needs: The quest for knowledge and meaning.
6. Aesthetic Needs: The pursuit of beauty, balance, and form.
7. Self-Actualization: Initially the highest level of Maslow's hierarchy of needs, self-actualization is where you focus on personal growth and fulfilling your potential.
8. Transcendence Needs: The need to help others to achieve self-actualization.

Maslow on self-actualization: "The specific form that these needs will take will of course vary greatly from person to person. In one individual it may take the form of the desire to be an ideal mother in another it may be expressed athletically, and still in another it may be expressed in painting pictures or in inventions" (Maslow, 1943).

Here are some classic cases where people failed to reach self-actualization and became chronically unhappy and even depressed: A star football player in high school injures himself and can't play ball anymore. A college student gets a girl pregnant, marries her, and has to drop out of college and get a job to support his family. A bright, ambitious, law student makes a mistake, gets in trouble with the law, gets a criminal record, and is unable to practice law.

Every person is capable of moving up the hierarchy to achieve the level of self-actualization, regardless of what has happened in the past. However, many people are precluded from reaching this level because of failure to meet lower level needs. Remember, you must satisfy lower level basic needs before progressing on to meet higher level growth needs.

Count Your Blessings

"I complained that I had no shoes, until I met someone who had no feet." —Unknown

Whenever something bad happens in my life, the first thing I say is, "It could have been worse." Things can always be worse. To count your blessings is a part of being positive. It means to be thankful for what you do have and not dwell on what you don't have. To count your blessings also means to be cognizant of others who are less fortunate than you. If you are alive, there is always someone worse off than you. I really believe if you do not appreciate what you do have, you will lose it. Conversely, be thankful for what you do have and you will get more. Give thanks for what you have, and give thanks in advance for what you want. It is a good habit to start your day with feeling blessed.

"The things we take for granted, someone else is praying for." —Unknown

You can always find something to be thankful for. Start with being thankful for being alive. Moreover, if you focus on what is good in your life, this will keep you from feeling unhappy. Gratitude helps keep your mind focused on the positive rather than the negative. If you need a thousand dollars, start by being thankful for the one hundred dollars you do have. When you focus on the one hundred you do have, it should be a reminder of the part of your life that is working, and a reminder of how you have already been blessed. This will encourage you. When you focus on what you have, you will receive more.

Not counting your blessings is limiting and can act as a barrier to greater things. People who see the glass half-empty instead of half-full are negative people. When you permit your thoughts to dwell on not having enough, you will experience not having enough. If you believe the glass is half-full, then you also believe that it can become full. Believe that you are blessed and see the glass as half-full.

> "I know both how to be abased, and I know how to abound: everywhere and in all things I am instructed both to be full and to be hungry, both to abound and to suffer need. I can do all things through Christ which strengtheneth me."
> —Philippians 4:12–13

You must learn how to face any situation, whether you are doing without or you have plenty. You must humble yourself in either situation. When things are not going so well, you must find the strength within to be self sufficient. Look for the answers within and tap into your infinite power through the power of God. Above all, be thankful for what you have.

I grew up in an affluent home, went to college, then went to law school. I experienced success early on in my career. I had my own law firm, other business interests, and was living a very good life. I had expensive homes and luxury cars. I wore designer clothes and ate at fancy restaurants. I didn't know what poverty was. Wealth was a way of life. I would tell people things were so good I could just pick money up off the sidewalks. I had it all. Unfortunately, I took all this for granted.

As a matter of fact, there was a time that I thought everyone owned a Mercedes or other luxury car. Then, out of the blue, everything changed. The bottom fell out of the market. My clients became insolvent and could no longer pay me. Like many others, I lost everything. I took for granted the riches that I already possessed in my life. This was my wake-up call. I decided then not to ever take anything for granted and to appreciate whatever I have, whether a little or a lot. It is easier to give thanks when you are doing well. However, it can be a challenge to give thanks for what you have when things are not going so well. The key is to give thanks not only for what you do have, but to also give thanks for the things you hope for.

Counting your blessings is essentially about gratitude. It is widely accepted that if you have abundance, and you do not show gratitude, you will eventually lose it. This is because you are intrinsically declaring to your subconscious mind (God, the universe) that you do not deserve it, and this will cancel out your manifestation. Accordingly, if you lack abundance, but show gratitude for what you do have, your subconscious mind (God, the universe) will consequently give you more of what you desire.

The more grateful we are when good things happen for us,
the more good things will happen.

Gratitude thinking has a very high-energy vibration. Gratitude goes beyond saying thank you. You must demonstrate gratitude in three ways. Firstly, express gratitude for what you already have. Secondly, express gratitude in advance for what you want. For example if you want a new house, give thanks in advance as though you have already received it. Thirdly, express gratitude by giving of yourself or your time to others.

"In everything give thanks"—1 Thessalonians 5:18

Make a habit of being grateful for everything. No matter how bad you think your life is, there is always something to be grateful for. Moreover, gratitude amplifies the law of attraction. Thus, what you receive through the law of attraction will be equal to the amount of gratitude you have demonstrated. Pay special attention to this point. This is a nuance that most people miss.

Lack of gratitude tends to impact one's life and lifestyle negatively. Complaining is the inverse of gratitude. Hence, gratitude creates wealth, and complaining creates poverty. Furthermore, the more effort you put into demonstrating gratitude, the more positive your results will be. It is a good habit to say thank you as many times a day as you can. Include in your prayers gratitude for what you desire or expect, as this will facilitate its manifestation.

Do Not Judge, Or You Too Will Be Judged

"JUDGE not, that ye be not judged. For with what judgment ye judge, ye shall be judged: and with what measure ye mete, it shall be measured to you again." —Matthew 7:1–2

To judge another is to criticize and condemn another. The law of attraction mandates that whatever you put out in the universe, you get back. Therefore, if you judge others, you will be judged, and you will be judged by the same measure that you have judged others. Therefore, if you judge harshly, you too will be judged harshly.

The concept of judging others is oftentimes misconstrued. In certain circumstances you may have the right to make objective judgments. Examples of this would be grading a student's paper or giving a verdict on a jury. But you must have the right to make this type of judgment, must have all the facts available to make a judgment, and you must be objective.

The judgments that we do not have the right to make and should not make are subjective judgments. When you judge, you are forming an opinion, and opinions are oftentimes formed from ignorance, fear, or pride. Judgments are intrinsically opinionated because they are subjective in nature.

"But with me it is a very small thing that I should be judged of you, or of man's judgment: yea, I judge not mine own self. For I know nothing by myself; yet am I not hereby justified: but he that judgeth me is the Lord." —1 Corinthians 4:3–4

Criticizing and condemning another is the type of judgment that you do not have the right to do. This type of judgment is the antithesis of love.

This type of judgment is inherently hypocritical, self-righteous, malicious, and destructive. This type of judgment is what is used to put people down. This is the type of judgment the Bible makes reference to. You can still hold people accountable for their actions without being judgmental. Let go, and let God do his job.

> "Speak not evil one of another, brethren. He that speaketh evil of *his* brother, and judgeth his brother, speaketh evil of the law, and judgeth the law: but if thou judge the law, thou art not a doer of the law, but a judge. There is one lawgiver, who is able to save and to destroy: who art thou that judgest another?" —James 4:11–12

Be mindful that if you judge another, you are actually sitting in judgment of the law and not following the law. Remember that there is only one lawgiver and judge, and it is not you. You must not be presumptuous and pass judgment on another. Also, be mindful that you should not judge another person, because you only have the ability to look at outward appearances and not the person's thoughts, experiences, and intentions. Only God knows each person's heart. There is no way you can know what is in a person's heart. Therefore, attributing spurious motives to other people is perverse, and no one has the right to do so except God. Wrongfully judging others is also a form of attack. Attacks on others are oftentimes precipitated by misconstruing others' character, motives, actions, and thinking.

> "Don't judge another man unless you have walked a mile in his shoes"—believed to have originated from a Native American proverb

You should not judge others' mistakes, unless you have walked a mile in their shoes. You think that you can know vicariously what another person experiences, feels, or thinks, but you can never really know. You don't know how you will act or react in another person's situation, unless you are in the exact same situation, with the exact same circumstances. In other words, you would have to actually be that person. Since this is impossible, this means that you should *never* judge another for their actions. We can *never* walk in another persons' shoes, not even if we walked for one hundred miles.

If you have made mistakes in your life, how can you judge others who have also made mistakes? Who are you to judge that your mistakes are less egregious than theirs?

Another reason why you should not judge another person is that when you judge another person, you are precluded from really helping that person. Making chastising or moralistic judgments implies that you feel superior to that person. This is because when you judge, you're focusing on the perceived negative of that person and not on helping that person. Your feelings of superiority and negativity will impede the compassion generally prerequisite to helping someone. Hence, you cannot really help people in need with a judgmental attitude.

Do not judge others as if you are superior to them.

"And why beholdest thou the mote that is in thou brother's eye, but perceivest not the beam that is in thine own eye? Either how canst thou say to thy brother, Brother, let me pull out the mote that is in thine eye, when thou thyself beholdest not the beam that is in thine own eye? Thou hypocrite, cast out first the beam out of thy own eye, and then shalt thou see clearly to pull out the mote that is in thy brother's eye." — Luke 6:41–42

It is clearly easier to criticize others' mistakes than to recognize your own. Instead of focusing on others' imperfections, you should focus instead on self-improvement. Being harshly critical of the mistakes and imperfections of others while tolerating and absolving your own is hypocrisy. Judging others is hypocritical because it signifies that the one judging is somehow exonerated from making mistakes and having imperfections. Hypocritical criticism is when criticism is used to tear others down in order to build oneself up.

We are all imperfect people, and imperfect people have no right to judge other imperfect people.

"Judging a person does not define who they are. It defines who you are."—Unknown

Judge people's situations, rather than judging the person. Whenever possible, don't judge a person by his acts alone. People tend to slander peoples' character based on a mistake or mistakes they've made. For example, people are quick to judge people in prison by their acts. I hear people referring to those who are in prison, or who have been in prison, as criminals. People are not their crimes; they are not their mistakes; they are not their failures; they are not their weaknesses; they are not their transgressions; and they are not their past. Moreover, always be cognizant of the universal law of oneness. Remember that we are all a part of one universal spirit, and you should treat your neighbor as you would treat yourself. Also, remember that you yourself will be judged by the one and only judge. You will ultimately be judged for wrongly judging others.

When we release judgment of others we release judgment of ourselves.

If you feel anger, resentment, and frustration toward a person, these are signs that you may be judging them. Insecurities and jealousy are oftentimes at the root of negatively judging others. Forgiveness and judgment of others are interrelated. Forgiveness involves the complete abatement of judgment. Judgment of others can also be a result of the blame game. It is a way of deflecting and blaming others for our faults, problems, and mistakes. Avoid playing the blame game by avoiding the passing of wrongful judgment on others. Instead deal with your own faults, problems, and mistakes. Some people judge others as a way of dominating them. Severely judgmental people have an inclination toward arrogance and tend to think they know it all. Judgmental people also tend to project negative attributes onto others that they don't like in themselves.

Ways to avoid being judgmental:

- Do not assess others based on your own mentality and outlook;
- Desist trusting second-hand information, gossip, or assumptions;
- Always give people the benefit of the doubt;

- Avoid rejecting people because of their past transgressions;
- Do not gage the reactions of others by your own predispositions;
- Do not reject someone simply because you do not understand them.

In short, do not wrongfully judge others.

The Power of Forgiveness

"For if ye forgive men their trespasses, your heavenly Father will also forgive you: But if ye forgive not men their trespasses, neither will your Father forgive your trespasses."
—Matthew 6: 14–15

If you let go of ill feelings toward others, thereby forgiving them when they commit wrongful acts against you, God will forgive you. Conversely, if you do not forgive others when they commit wrongful acts against you, God will not forgive you.

Un-forgiveness is actually *de facto* hatred towards another. Based on the universal law of oneness, if you hate another, you are hating yourself. Being unable to forgive affects your health, your relationships with others, and how you view the world. More importantly, un-forgiveness will preclude God from forgiving your sins. In point of fact, forgiveness has absolutely nothing to do with other people. It has everything to do with the individual giving the forgiveness. In actuality, it is something we do for ourselves. When you forgive others, you remove barriers to receiving goodness into your life. If someone has done you wrong or you perceive that someone has done you wrong, you must forgive them for your own sake.

Sometimes hurtful and bad things are done to us or someone we love. Sometimes we recover from this completely. Sometimes it takes a long time. Sometimes we are able to recover partially. Sometimes we never recover. Almost always, it takes forgiveness of others to recover, and sometimes it takes forgiving ourselves. Forgiveness is empowering and is essential to having peace of mind.

"And forgive us our debts, as we forgive our debtors"
—Matthew 6:12

Forgiveness does not mean that you condone the grievous act or acts done by others. Nor does it undo the past. Forgiving someone doesn't mean that transgressors will not pay for what they have done. It is not for us to worry about whether they will pay. That is God's job. They will pay according to the law of retribution. The law of retribution mandates that for every wrong we do, we will pay a cost and will have to make amends. It promulgates that we will pay for our wrongs in one way or another, in this lifetime or the next. Forgiving another person for the wrongs we believe they did to us is a form of retribution. To forgive another is tantamount to asking for forgiveness for the wrongs we have committed. In other words, if you don't forgive another, you will suffer the consequences of the law of retribution.

"Ye have heard that it hath been said, An eye for an eye, and a tooth for a tooth: But I say unto you, That ye resist not evil: but whoever shall smite thee on thy right cheek, turn to him the other also."—Matthew 5: 38-39

Many people erroneously believe literally in the eye-for-an-eye edict. The references in the Bible to "an eye for an eye" is the antithesis of forgiveness. It is also the antithesis of Matthew 5:38–39. In fact, in Matthew 5:38–39, the incongruity is corrected. The eye-for-an-eye edict was a figurative command in the Old Testament and was not to be taken literally. It was a civil law decree intended to make justice equitable, and it related to the repayment of wrongs in the form of goods. This eye-for-an-eye mandate was intended as guidance for the courts and not intended to apply to personal relationships. It has been well established that this law was not to be literally executed.

You can't correct a negative action with another negative action.

"Holding on to anger is like drinking poison and expecting the other person to die."—Buddha

Many people are under the misconception that the other person suffers when they hold a grudge against another. In fact, if you don't forgive the person and forget the wrong, you will be the person hurt. It is in your own best interest to forgive others. When you don't forgive, you are imprisoned by the negative feelings you harbor. You remain emotionally shackled to them. By forgiving another, you essentially free yourself. Moreover, when you forgive another, you will release the anger, hatred, and resentment. You will allow healing to take place. Stop trying to hurt people that hurt you. Forgive them, let them go, and move on with your own life.

Forgiveness will set you free.

Harboring negative emotions, affects your mental and physical health. It sometimes affects your self-esteem, your ability to love, to be loved, and to be compassionate. It may also be a road block to your success and happiness in life. There is no healing, no recovery, and no re-building until these feelings are dealt with. Therefore, do not ignore your feelings of anger, resentment, hatred, and so on. If you don't admit to being hurt or angry and don't express your anger in constructive ways, you may destroy significant relationships.

"Let all bitterness, and wrath, and anger, and clamour, and evil speaking, be put away from you, with all malice: And be ye kind one to another, even as God for Christ's sake hath forgiven you." —Ephesians 4:31–32

"I, *even* I, *am* he that blotteth out thy transgressions for mine own sake, and will not remember thy sins."—Isaiah 43:25

It is a very hard thing to do, but for your own good you must rid yourself of all feelings of resentment, hostility, and animosity. Instead you must show compassion, kindness, and understanding. This is the embodiment of forgiveness.

I counseled a woman named Gloria, who had led a very tumultuous life. She was raped at the age of six, and molested for many years by her father. Having grown up on the streets of a small city in Colombia, as an adult she had a tough façade. However she was not tough at all.

She was quite fragile emotionally and said she cried all the time when alone. Suffering from depression, she tried to kill herself on at least three occasions. To make matters worse, she was addicted to crack cocaine, and had diabetes. She also had a long history of trouble with the law. She had spent many years hating her father, and most men.

Gloria, like so many people who have had difficult lives, was consumed with negative emotions. These negative emotions got in the way of her living a positive life. I asked her if she had forgiven her father. She said no, that she could never forgive him. Although he had died, I explained to her how important it was to forgive him and forget the wrong he had done to her. That was the only way she could make room for positive things to happen in her life.

Gloria said she would forgive him, but she would never forget. Many people make this mistake. In order to truly forgive, you must also forget. *Forgiven* means that a debt or liability has been cancelled. "I can forgive, but I can't forget," is just a different way of saying: "I won't forgive". Moreover, if you don't forget, you will not be able to make a positive move forward. Forgiveness and forgetting are both necessary for healing and moving forward.

To forgive and remember leads to more conflict; to forgive and forget leads to more love.

There are consequences to living with an unforgiving heart. Unforgiveness is like a small wound that turns into a horrific infection that gets worse and worse as you pick at it. It is like a sore that never heals. Like the infected wound, your life becomes worse and worse, and you become more and more unhappy and bitter.

We do not have the right to choose which transgressions are forgivable and which are not. To do so would require wrongful judging of another, which only God has the right to do. Furthermore, there is no act, no crime, and no wrong that is too heinous for forgiveness. This means that forgiveness must extend to the man who raped you, the parent that abandoned you, the person who murdered your child, and the spouse that betrayed you.

Sometimes people don't forgive others because they don't feel they deserve forgiveness. Again, this is making a wrongful judgment, as only

God can make that judgment. Furthermore, God forgives you all the time, whether you deserve it or not. Therefore, forgive everyone, always, for everything.

Some people use forgiveness to make themselves feel better, thinking they are giving someone a gift they do not deserve. In fact, all people are worthy of forgiveness, and it is you who will receive a gift by forgiving another. Forgiveness is a gift we give ourselves, as it gives us peace.

You must forgive everyone who has ever hurt you if you want perfect health and happiness. If you really think about how much God has forgiven you in your lifetime, the revelation will far outweigh the wrongs done against you. Yet, you are not willing to forgive? God promises not only to forgive your sins, but to forget them as well. Although it may be difficult, you need only decide to be forgiving. Don't make an apology or contrition a pre-requisite to forgiveness. That's just an excuse not to forgive. You cannot evolve without forgiveness of others. Forgiveness leads to peace and spiritual growth.

Forgiveness is a sign of strength, not a sign of weakness.

It is also important to forgive yourself. If there is something that you have done wrong or badly, or you have hurt someone, forgive yourself. Otherwise it is probably preventing you from having something, achieving something, attaining something, or being something. You can feel guilty about your thoughts as well as your actions. For example, hoping that someone has misfortune, pain, or maybe even death. You may even feel guilty about feelings of hatred, resentment, and jealousy toward another. You may need to determine what you actually feel guilty about in order to move forward.

Guilt and un-forgiveness of the self can be self-destructive. Guilt will destroy your confidence. It will make you feel insecure because you will be worried that someone is going to find out what you've done or what kind of person you really are. Forgiveness of oneself is essential to letting go of guilt and moving on with your life.

Self-forgiveness is also essential to having fulfilling relationships and self-acceptance and esteem. Guilt causes self-anger, loathing, and resentment. Furthermore, it will cause anger, loathing, and resentment toward others, as a way of validating your wrongdoing. Guilt can damage and even destroy relationships. When we live with un-absolved issues we are likely to react to people in perverse ways, like being impatient, angry, or alienating oneself from family and friends. Guilt can lead to depression and other mental illnesses as well.

It is equally as important that you earnestly ask for forgiveness from those you have wronged. This acts as a purifier of your soul, and will assist you in your journey toward enlightenment.

How to get rid of guilt:

- Take responsibility for what you did, said, or thought;
- Identify your motives for doing it;
- Determine what lesson(s) were learned or should have been learned;
- Write yourself a letter of forgiveness;
- Affirm that you forgive yourself;
- Pray for the ability to be free of the guilt.

Why you may find forgiveness difficult:

- You think that an eye for an eye is justifiable;
- You think you are punishing the transgressor by withholding forgiveness;
- You want the transgressor to feel pain as you have;
- You're angry, and it's difficult to forgive someone if you are angry with them;
- You don't believe that the transgressor deserves to be forgiven;
- You lack compassion for your transgressor;
- You're waiting for an apology or for the person to own up to their transgression;
- You can't get past seeing the transgressor as their transgression, and you are unwilling to acknowledge that person as a human being with any good qualities.

Five step process to forgiving and releasing negative emotions:

1. Write down the cause of and acknowledge your negative emotions. Then, in a relaxed atmosphere, verbalize your acknowledgement of your particular negative emotions. For example: "I am angry with my mother for…" "I resent my wife for…" "I hate my boyfriend for…" "I feel guilty about…" "I sometimes feel angry when other people…"
2. You then have to do something affirmative to get rid of these negative emotions. Whatever you wrote down, take the paper and burn it or tear it up. Then verbalize the following: "I get rid of the anger I have toward my mother, and I forgive her for…" "I burn up my resentment for my wife, and I forgive her for…" "I release the hatred I have for my boyfriend, and I forgive him for…" "I tear up these guilty feelings I have concerning…, and I forgive myself." I will no longer get angry when other people…; my anger is going up in smoke." Another way to deal with negative emotions toward someone is to constructively express your feelings to the object of your negativity. If you cannot express your feelings face to face, you might write a letter to the person who has wronged you.
3. You may talk things out with someone. This person may be a friend or they may be a counselor or other mental health professional. This is a healthy release of feelings.
4. Pray. Pray for help in forgiveness and releasing negative emotions and feelings. Also, pray for those who have wronged you.
5. Forgive and forget. Actively give up your grudge, despite the severity of the injustice you perceive has been done to you. Then forget about it.

Leave the Past in the Past

"Avoid the trap of looking back –

Unless it's to recall a lesson learned

Or to glory in what God has accomplished." —Unknown

There are only two things one should hold on to from the past: lessons learned, and gratitude that the past brought you to where you are now. If you have your mind focused on the past, and relive it over and over, whatever negative experience you had will become a part of you. Many people revisit the bad things that have happened in the past, and they continue to be victims. Any part of your past that negatively influences your present becomes a part of your present. Stop holding on to past experiences that are no longer relevant to your life. Holding on to negative experiences from the past will impede your progress in the present. Do not let what has happened to you in the past define who you are. Do not let the effects of old wounds become a part of your life.

Don't become your past.

Sometimes negative things that have happened to you in the past will overpower you. You will tend to hold on to them because you aren't able to comprehend them. You can't understand why someone would hurt, abandon, or betray you. Consequently, your heart becomes hardened and you don't want to forgive them, nor do you feel that you can. This will keep you living in the past. Holding on to the past is like being blind in one eye, and what you are able to see out of the other eye is clouded by the experiences of your past.

Negative emotions are a waste of time. They keep you dwelling in the past, which is counterproductive. People oftentimes use what happened in the past as an excuse for where they are presently. Alternatively, you can focus on what you really want out of life. Get rid of the baggage from the past, and you will open up new possibilities and opportunities to create a new and better future.

Life only moves in one direction—toward the future.

Many people stay in denial of negative emotions for most of their lives. Harboring negative emotions will have limiting and detrimental effects on your life. A lot of emotional, psychosomatic, and interpersonal problems are a result of harbored negative emotions. Negative emotions, whether repressed or not, can lead to problems such as, obesity, insomnia, fatigue, psychological disorders, and sexual problems.

Feelings like, anger, resentment, hatred, and guilt are heavy negative baggage. You carry around that baggage, it only weighs you down. Not many people remember the days before luggage was manufactured with wheels, and many do not remember the days before people-movers and trains were in airports. There was a time when you had to carry very heavy luggage for long distances through airports. Your arms would inevitably tire, and you would have to keep stopping to rest. The absolute worst experience was when you had to run to catch a plane with this heavy luggage on your shoulders. It is no different carrying heavy emotional luggage around through life.

Some people, who have not let go of the past and who hold on to negative emotions, are not aware or are in denial. These negative emotions are typically manifested through sulking, whining, cynicism, enviousness, sarcasm, bitterness, and martyr complexes. Yet other people, while not appearing to have these traits, are generally self-effacing, and generally shoulder the blame for the wrong done. This person may have psychosomatic complaints as an outlet for his or her negative emotions.

There is the person who takes the silent, icy approach to dealing with negative emotions. Then there is the passive-aggressive person, who is characterized by aggressive behavior exhibited in passive ways, such as pouting, stubbornness, and contrarianism. One of my husbands was this type. I would speak to him, and he would totally ignore me. He would never do anything that I asked. I knew that if I had a chance of getting anything done, I should not even ask. Moreover, he would always take an opposing view to mine. If I said the sky was clear, he would argue that the sky was gray. I could tell by how he spoke to me—with animosity and sometimes hostility—that he had a great deal of anger and resentment buried underneath his seemingly non-threatening façade.

Negativity attracts negativity. Pursuant to the law of attraction, holding on to negative emotions from the past will continue to attract negativity to your life. Pain and past hurts oftentimes cause social conflict in the present. Carrying anger, resentment, bitterness, and animosity from the past only hinders *you*—no one else. Holding on can also block blessings and opportunities. Therefore, you should check to see if you have emotionally shackled yourself to the past. If so, let go. Otherwise you are likely hurting yourself and others.

Nostalgia, living in the good ol' days and constantly yearning for the way things used to be, can also cheat you of new and better experiences in the present. The universe is constantly changing, you are constantly changing, and your life is constantly changing. Reliving the past takes up precious mental space in your life in the now.

Letting go of the past can be tough, whether it is letting go of bad habits, relationships, or feelings. It is easy to intellectualize letting go, but in many cases it is challenging to actually do.

Let go of the old and make way for the new.

Suggestions on how to let go of the past:

- Try to determine why you haven't been able to let go of the past.
- Take ownership of negative emotions you are carrying from the past like anger, resentment, hatred, and guilt.
- Release these negative emotions through affirmations.
- Let go of your victim story and take responsibility for your life. Stop blaming the past, or someone in your past, as no one else is responsible for you but you.
- Put your past situation into perspective.

- Be mindful of when you start to dwell in the past and replace these thoughts with other positive thoughts.
- Ritualize letting go of past pain. For example, write out your painful experience and feelings, then burn the paper, affirming that you release the pain.
- Focus on the present: your goals, aspirations, and purpose in life.
- Start moving forward by taking positive action toward your goals, aspirations, and life purpose.
- Love your life, and embrace your life now.
- Be grateful for where you are and what you have.
- Focus on helping others, particularly others that are in similar situations to those you were once in.
- Seek professional help if you are unable to help yourself: join a support group or get therapy.
- Seek spiritual guidance and comfort.
- Meditate and pray. "Lord, I surrender my heart to you. I give you all my disappointments, pain, and sufferings, which only you can understand. Please give me the strength to let go of the past and move forward."

Funny How Time Slips Away

Carpe diem is Latin for *seize the day*, and is taken to mean *live in the moment*. It originated in a poem by Horace. The poem advocates that since the future is unknown and you should not leave future happenings to chance, you should do all that you can do today to make your future better. Make the most of *now*. You can only take one breath at a time, and that time is *now*. The only breath that matters is the breath you are taking now. There is only *now*. The choices you make now will impact your future, which is tomorrow's *now*. Some people use the concept to justify reckless behavior. They misinterpret its meaning as, "You only live once." This doesn't mean to ignore the lessons of the past or not to prepare for the future. The caveat is to appreciate being alive *now*.

Learn from the past, prepare for the future, but live for today.

If we withdraw ourselves from the past and the future, we free up creative energy that we normally imprison in the past or the future. If you live in the now, you will therefore be much more creative and productive. Instead of worrying about the past or the future, just be alive. To be alive entails much more than simply breathing. Being alive means to feel happy, energized, vibrant, and excited.

"Today is the first day of the rest of your life."—Unknown

Start living in the moment. Don't think about the past, what ifs, or the good ol' days. The key to living in the now is to shed all guilt and all regrets. Do not cling to the past. When we cling to the past we are not totally available to the present. Take one day at a time. Not only that, but take one moment at a time. Discover the beauty of living in the moment.

Consider how you would spend your time if you had one month to live. Is there a dream or a goal that you have been putting off?

Living in the moment is not the same as living for the moment.

Sometimes we do too much and allow time to escape unobtrusively. When you're always doing something like working, taking care of children, studying, building a business, and so on, you're not taking advantage of the moment. Sometimes we must be still and take in life. Watch a sun set, smell a rose, or breathe in some fresh mountain air. Take daily vacations during which you don't think about work or problems. Instead, focus on beauty, nature, and living in the now.

Tomorrow, today will be gone forever.

Most mornings I sit on my front porch at my country home, drink coffee, watch the squirrels play, listen to the birds, gaze at the lush green trees, and think to myself, "Life doesn't get any better than this." This daily vacation doesn't cost me anything. It also puts me in a good frame of mind to face the challenges of the day. This scenario is a huge departure from earlier days. I actually spent more than twenty years doing nothing but working and focusing on making money. Don't get me wrong, making money has its upside, and there's nothing wrong with being driven. However, you have to remember to live a balanced life.

While making a living, don't forget to live.

On the opposite end of the spectrum to those that do too much, there are those that do too little. There are those that spend too much time deciding, planning, contemplating, and procrastinating. All the while they are doing nothing, life is happening. Even if you are going through hard times, it's the only time you presently have, so do not squander it. Begin doing what you need or want to do now, as you only have the present moment to begin doing it.

Lost time can never be found.

Step back and look at the big picture of your life. Living a balanced life is part of living in the now. Life is multi-dimensional. A well-balanced life entails spending time on family, friends, work, physical and mental health, leisure and enjoyment, love, personal growth and spirituality, learning and intellectual growth, socializing, and financial well-being. Recognize and give time to the important dimensions of your life. Plan, prepare, and make time for these neglected dimensions. Determine what dimensions of your life need more attention and remove those that need less attention. The more balanced and well-rounded your life is, the happier you will be. If your life is out of balance, you may feel overwhelmed, anxious, worried, frustrated, lonely, and powerless. You may also suffer from low self-esteem or self-confidence.

Tips for living a balanced life:

- Make note of neglected areas of your life.
- Decide on how you will get more balance in your life.
- Take some “me time” or relaxation time every day.
- Exercise.
- Eat right.
- Do everything in moderation.
- Rejuvenate your body nightly by getting sufficient rest.
- Manage your time. Plan and prepare in advance for things that need to be done as well as things you want to do.
- Stay connected with family and friends.
- Don’t bite off more than you can chew. Prioritize and focus, and avoid becoming overwhelmed.
- Adopt the mindset of making the most of each day. Live in and savor as many moments as possible.
- Find ways to reduce stress.
- Periodically spend time on a hobby you enjoy, or learn a new hobby.
- Work on furthering your education or enhancing your skills.
- Find something to laugh about.
- Commune with nature: take hikes, go camping, go fishing.
- Be your own best friend.

- Find time to help others.
- Don't focus too much on making money.
- Pray, meditate and visualize daily.

Today will never come again.

What's Love Got to Do With It?

"Charity suffereth long, *and* is kind; charity envieth not; charity vaunteth not itself, is not puffed up, Doth not behave itself unseemly, seeketh not her own, is not easily provoked, thinketh no evil; Rejoiceth not in iniquity, but rejoiceth in the truth; Beareth all things, believeth all things, hopeth all things, endureth all things."—1 Corinthians 13:4–7

What's love got to do with it? Love has *everything* to do with *everything*! Love is the cause of everything, of all creation. Love incarnates itself. To love means that you wish happiness, health, peace, joy, the best that life has to offer, and blessings for others. Love is being kind and patient towards others. It is not rude, selfish, spiteful, jealous, arrogant, or proud. Love does not envy or boast. Nor, is it easy to anger. Love trusts, protects, and forgives. Love is hope, perseverance, and truth. Love endures.

Love means determining what is best for another person and then doing it.

The great thing about love is that if you give it, you will receive it. Love is the greatest power in the universe. Love is God. Love involves understanding, benevolence, and respect for the divinity in all humankind. The more you love and wish benevolence to others, the more of the same will return to you. So give love and benevolence, and it will be returned to you. On the other hand, if you attack another person or are unkind to them, you cannot gain their benevolence. Everyone seeks to be loved and appreciated. Above all, you cannot gain happiness through the unhappiness of others. This law of love is universal, which means it applies to everyone, everywhere, and under every circumstance.

Self-interest is not present in universal love (also known as *divine love* and *agape love*). Universal Love is altruistic, giving and not expecting anything in return. However, by virtue of one's desire to advance the happiness and well-being of others, one actually advances the happiness and well-being of the universal mind (God). Therefore, you circuitously advance your own happiness and well-being. Moreover, universal love transcends all social, economic, racial, and religious characteristics.

Be in love with the world.

"And thou shalt love the Lord thy God with all thy heart, and with all thy soul, and with all thy mind, and with all thy strength: this *is* the first commandment. And the second *is* like, *namely* this, Thou shalt love thy neighbor as thyself". There is none other commandment greater than these."— Mark 12:30–1

The two greatest commandments, which are considered the nucleus of the Christian religion, underscore how important Love is. Agape (divine and universal) love is the love of God for humankind. It is the highest and purist form of love, unconditional and unselfish. To reach this level of love, you must not engage your feelings and you must give love unselfishly. The highest good is in giving, not in receiving. This means to love others as God loves you. To advance towards unconditional love, you must become accustomed to thinking, speaking, and acting as God would. Agape love is crucial to reaching higher consciousness and spiritual enlightenment. The concept of universal love must become a part of who you are in order to advance to a higher consciousness and spiritual enlightenment.

To reach higher consciousness and spiritual enlightenment, love others as God loves you.

"Love points the way and the Law makes the thing possible."—Ernest Holmes

Most importantly, without the influence of universal (agape) love, the law of attraction and the law of abundance cannot work in your favor. Universal love is the key to everything and should be one's ultimate goal in life. Therefore to get love, happiness, health, peace, joy, blessings, and the best life has to offer, love others as God loves you. Remember that God's love is also total forgiveness and devoid of judgment.

> Judge no one. Think good of everyone. Forgive everyone.
> Bless everyone. Serve others unselfishly. Wish for everyone
> what you wish for yourself. Love everyone. This is love.

Love puts you in a great emotional state. If you have negative thoughts such as hatred and resentment towards another person, you are the one harmed by these negative thoughts. Conversely if you have thoughts of love toward others, you'll benefit from it. This is because love gives power to thought.

It is important to maintain universal love, even when others are not kind and compassionate to you. Always show love to others in the way you think, speak, and act towards them. Universal love for others means that you must rise above emotion and ego, and learn to see others in a different light. You must see them as connected spirits. When you are able to do this, you will find that universal love will penetrate all areas of your life, and life will be good.

It is difficult to love others if you do not love yourself. This is because it is difficult to wish happiness, health, peace, joy, blessings, and the best that life has to offer for others if you yourself do not wish the same for yourself. Perhaps you do not feel you deserve to be happy. Perhaps you feel you are not worthy of the best that life has to offer. Loving oneself means to respect oneself as a creation of God. God commanded us to love one another as we love ourselves. Hence, if you do not love yourself, you cannot love others.

> "Finally, brethren, whatsoever things are true, whatsoever
> things *are* honest, whatsoever things *are* just, whatsoever
> things *are* pure, whatsoever things *are* lovely, whatsoever
> things *are* of good report; if *there be* any virtue, and if
> *there be* any praise, think on these things. Those things,
> which ye have both learned, and received, and heard,

> and seen in me, do: and the God of Peace shall be with you."—Philippians 4:8–9

Good, virtuous, honest, noble, kind, and compassionate thoughts and feelings are the essence of love. We are meant to emulate what we have experienced and learned from God. If we do this, we will find inner peace. We are motivated by the feelings of love we experience when we have things like the perfect job, the perfect mate, the perfect body, perfect health, and more than enough money. To attract these things, according to the law of attraction, we must have thoughts and feelings of love. The catch-22 is that you have to love yourself first before you can have these thoughts and feelings of love. To love yourself you must first realize that your inner self is perfect. Understand that we are all God manifested in human form. This means that by nature you are perfect, powerful, loving, infinitely intelligent, and happy. To help you become outwardly what your inner self is, affirm regularly, "I am perfect, powerful, loving, infinitely intelligent, and happy." Love yourself!

> "Therefore all things whatsoever ye would that men should do to you, do ye even so to them: for this is the law and the prophets."—Matthew 7:12

Do unto others what you would have them do unto you. This exemplifies the principle of brotherly love, the golden rule, the law of Moses, and it is a corollary of the law of attraction. The golden rule: treat others as you would like others to treat you. The golden rule is an integral part of many cultures and religions, and it is fundamental to prosperity and successful living.

The golden rule extends its meaning to: Be kind to those that are unkind to you. It means to put to shame those people who mean harm or do harm to you, by showing them kindness in return. It extends to enemies as well. If you attempt to gain happiness at the expense of others' happiness, happiness will evade you. Some believe that the golden rule is a doctrine of reciprocity, but in actuality it is not. Rather it represents outright altruism and unmitigated love.

Only through brotherly love, will you truly have peace.
Always return violence and hatred with peacefulness and love.

"*Let* love be without dissimulation. Abhor that which is evil; cleave to that which is good. *Be* kindly affectioned one to another with brotherly love; in honour preferring one another"—Romans 12:9–10

Be sincere and put yourself in another's place. Do not inflict upon others the pain and suffering that you yourself hate. In other words, do not do things to others that you know cause pain and suffering. Moreover, take any opportunity to use what you have to help others. Be devoted to others as if they were members of your family. Hold others in high esteem. It is not enough to merely refrain from harming others. You must be proactive in assisting others.

As pain is not agreeable to you, it is not agreeable to others.
So, do not inflict pain on others.

"And above all things have fervent charity among yourselves: for charity shall cover the multitude of sins. Use hospitality one to another without grudging. As every man hath received the gift, *even so* minister the same one to another, as good stewards of the manifold grace of God."—1 Peter 4:8–10

A significant life lesson to learn is to realize that we are one with God and our souls connect. We are connected to each other and to God (supreme being, universe, the source, universal mind, universal consciousness). You are your brother, and your brother is you. Treat your brothers with love, compassion, and understanding. Hating others, being cruel to others, and judging others is the same as hating yourself, being cruel to yourself, and judging yourself. Even when you verbally abuse, physically abuse, criticize, or put someone down, you are affecting yourself negatively. When you alienate yourself from others, you are alienating yourself from God. Accordingly, every time you do for another, you are doing for yourself and for the oneness that you are a part of. Whatever good deeds you do for another, you're ultimately doing for yourself. When you truly understand this, you will love everyone because you will become the essence of love. When you become enlightened, you will treat others as you want to be treated. You will show compassion to others. You will forgive others. You will not judge others.

Science supports the principle of oneness. Einstein's $E=mc^2$ theory essentially states that everything is energy and all energy is connected. This means that everything exists within oneness (also referred to as god, universal mind, universal consciousness, supreme being) and is also connected to the oneness. In other words, our subconscious minds are connected. Our lives appear to be separate, but they are not. We are not separate parts of a whole; rather, we are a whole. The fundamental quality of this oneness is unlimited power through love. Therefore, we should be a light for others in times of need and help others whenever we can.

I Feel Your Pain—Compassion for Others

"Remember them that are in bonds, as bound with them; *and* them which suffer adversity, as being yourselves also in the body."—Hebrews 13:3

Compassion means to care about others and to bless others. It is to have understanding and to be forgiving. Compassion is demonstrating God's mercy and love to others in need. The need could be financial, spiritual, emotional, or material. Give an encouraging word to someone who is depressed, give money to someone out of work, or just show kindness and support. Compassion entails vicariously experiencing the feelings, thoughts, and experience of another person and being understanding and sensitive to their plight. Even if you haven't had the same experience, put yourself into their shoes. For instance, instead of looking down on those in prison, feel their pain as if you yourself were in prison. Instead of ignoring those that are mistreated, feel their pain as if you, yourself were being mistreated. It is not enough to feel this way. You must reach out and convey your empathy to them in some manner.

I remember approximately twenty years ago, I was changing planes at Heathrow Airport in London. For some reason, I couldn't make my connecting flight to South Africa. Others were unable to make their connections as well. There were a lot of upset people, and there was one lady in particular who was crying hysterically. After observing her for a while, I finally went over and asked her what was troubling her. She was beside herself, but I finally got out of her that she was afraid and didn't know what to do. She was travelling alone, as was I. I told her we couldn't get a flight out until the morning, so she should go to a hotel for the night.

She didn't want to leave the airport. I had planned on going to the hotel, but I couldn't bring myself to leave her. So I gave her a hug and told her that everything would be okay and that I would stay with her at the airport overnight. I let her call her husband on my cell phone. I then gave her my airline blanket. We slept on the floor of the airport side by side that night. It was cold and uncomfortable, but I knew I couldn't leave her. I actually woke up with a cold and not feeling well, so I saw her to her plane, and I returned to New York.

Five years later I was going through a rough period in my life, and I was changing planes at Heathrow Airport again. Feeling dejected, I was thinking about my troubles as tears welled up in my eyes. A stranger walked up behind me and put her arm around me, squeezed me, and told me everything would be okay. When she touched me a very warm sensation ran through my body and I immediately felt better. She turned and walked away without another word. Mind you she never saw the tears in my eyes. It was as if a heavy burden had been lifted, and I no longer had a heavy heart.

You see? Whatever you give will be given back to you. Show beneficence toward others and it will return to enhance your own life in ways you cannot foresee. Bless others and you will be blessed. These are principles that you should live by. These principles also mean that you cannot treat others badly and expect to be blessed. Help others with broken hearts, dreams, and spirits. Show compassion for those who are worse off than you. You cannot really help another person unless you have compassion for that person. It is when we understand people and the genesis of their problems that we become compassionate, sympathetic, and patient with them.

> "Be not forgetful to entertain strangers: for thereby some have entertained angels unawares." —Hebrews 13:2

Carla, another woman I counseled, had many gifts and a superb intellect. She counseled and ministered to other women who were in trouble. I was in awe of her because she showed a lot of compassion for other women that were incarcerated as she was. I know from our talks that Carla had an extremely difficult life. She lived with the knowledge that she was a product of incest; her grandfather molested her mother. She was molested herself at an early age. At the time she was a prostitute and had been near death many times. She had been hungry and homeless many times as well. Carla probably spent more time in jail than out of it, but she had this unbelievable, amazing compassion for others. I referred to her as an angel that's a little rough around the wings.

You can stop showing compassion to others when God stops showing compassion to you.

Hope Springs Eternal

"But they that wait upon the LORD shall renew their strength; they shall mount up with wings like eagles; they shall run, and not be weary; *and* they will walk, and not faint."—Isaiah 40:31

Are you so beaten down by the troubles in your life that you have become discouraged? Maybe you've been through a lot of pain, disappointment, and misery, and you have tried and tried and nothing seems to change in your life. No matter how much suffering you have endured, you must not accept these conditions.

No matter the circumstances, and no matter how bad things have been, they can always get better. Do not give up hope that your life can change for the better. No matter how many disappointments you have endured, there is always hope. Feel it and believe it. When you are at a low point, this is the time to feed your mind with positive thoughts. Focusing on positive thoughts leads to hope. If you believe that you can accomplish positive change in your life, you will feel that there is hope.

Hope is the guiding light in the darkness, on the twists and turns of our journey called life.

"Hope is a waking dream" —Aristotle

Hope is much more than a feel-good emotion. If you have hope, you have the will and determination to set and achieve goals. Hope is important because it helps us navigate the rough waters on the sea of life.

If you have hope you understand that there are no unsolvable problems. If you have hope you understand that your broken heart, shattered dreams, and disappointments can be fixed.

Faith and hope are dissimilar. Faith is placing trust in that which you cannot see. Hope precedes faith. It is a driving force in believing that things can and will get better. It motivates us to do and have more. Hope is what gives life purpose. Without it, there is nothing to plan for or look forward to and thus, nothing to live for. For instance, there would be no point in going to school, if there was no hope of one day getting a good job or career as a result.

Dreams make us who we are. Hope is what fuels our dreams. Every great achievement started with a dream and was motivated by hope. We must always have hope. Without hope there is no happiness and nothing to look forward to. Hope is empowering. It is the vehicle that transitions one from anguish, pessimism, and despair to believing that life can be better.

"If we believe that tomorrow will be better, we can endure a hardship today."—Unknown

In life, one can easily lose hope. Humankind needs hope. Hope is vital to keep us going through hard times. It is the only thing that can pull us out of the depths of despair. We dream of something better than we presently have, and it is hope that pushes us to keep going. Hope is that light that you just know is on the other side of the dark tunnel. Hope is knowing that you will eventually step outside that tunnel and see light. The essence of hope is knowing that after the darkness there is always light. Therefore, if you have hope, you will be motivated, you will persevere, and you will endure. Having hope is like looking out an open window and knowing that you can climb out at anytime. It is knowing that your dire situation is not permanent. It is the expectation that things will change for the better despite challenging circumstances.

Never give up hope no matter how bad things may seem. The moment you give up hope, you lose.

Have Peace of Mind

"Blessed *is* the man that trusteth in the LORD, and whose hope the LORD is. For he shall be as a tree planted by the waters, and *that* spreadeth out her roots by the river, and shall not see when heat cometh, but her leaf shall be green; and shall not be careful in the year of drought, neither shall cease from yielding fruit."—Jeremiah 17:7–8

"I will both lay me down in peace, and sleep: for thou, LORD, only makest me dwell in safety." —Psalm 4:8

When you have peace of mind, you're able to sleep soundly. Peace of mind means you are confident with putting your trust in God. Whenever your spirit resides in peace, you will reside in peace. To have peace of mind doesn't mean the absence of trouble, calamity, or strife. It means to be engulfed in these things and still find serenity. It is living contentedly in ones' own moment while moving forward. It is contentment in knowing there is plenty available for everyone. Peace of mind is something that only you can attain. Your lover, your friends, and your family cannot give it to you. Many people spend their lives chasing material things and romantic love. None of these are permanent, and none can give you peace of mind. A peaceful mind can only be discovered from within, spiritually.

Peace of mind is serenity. Serenity is not shelter from the storm, but calmness amidst the storm.

Where and how do you find peace of mind?

The answer is spiritual in nature. The key is firstly to free yourself from conditions and circumstances that prevent you from finding peace of mind. Secondly, you must explore your spiritual nature. You must examine the relationship between your self and the universe (God; supreme being). You must acknowledge that you are a part of the universe and everything that exists, and that the universe is a part of you. In other words, you are universal in nature. Once you know and acknowledge the true relationship between your inner self and the universe, you will begin your journey towards peace of mind (inner peace). Thirdly, peace of mind is found in knowing and acknowledging that there are universal laws that affect you and everything in the universe. Finally, you must follow the universal laws in order to have peace of mind.

Since we are all connected and comprise this universe as one, our relationships with the rest of the world is fundamental to having peace of mind. Therefore you must resolve conflicts between yourself and others. You can do this by knowing you have the supreme power to think positively for the good of all. You must realize that you have the infinite power to create a positive life with positive thoughts. Furthermore, you are more apt to find peace of mind when you can roll with the punches. Accept that stuff happens, and know that you have the power of the universe at your disposal to help you deal with the negative stuff that happens in everyday life.

Peace of mind is a place found only inside of you.

Everyone is born with peace of mind. However, along the way, it can be lost. Just like happiness, we can have peace of mind if we make the decision to have it. When obstacles and problems happen many people erroneously believe they can regain peace of mind with the use of addictive substances. In fact, they end up achieving the opposite. Addiction is an example of people looking for answers outside of self instead of within. Inner peace of mind ultimately manifests into outer peace. By creating peace in your mind, you transfer it into your outer world, and into other peoples' lives.

Gratitude is a channel to finding peace of mind. Focusing on what you have and being thankful will lead you toward peace of mind. Peace of mind comes from accepting what you have at the time and being grateful for it. This doesn't negate having dreams and achieving goals. It's recognizing that no matter what, you always have something to be grateful for. Gratitude alters your focus from inadequacies in your life to the abundance that is already at your disposal.

"Be still, and know that I *am* God. "—Psalm 46:10

We can free ourselves from disquieting and disheartening thoughts and emotions by being still. Many times when we aren't voluntarily still, the universe (God; supreme being) will force us to be still by blocking us with circumstances such as illness, loss, or adverse change: circumstances that force us to stop and be still.

"For every minute that you remain angry, you give up sixty seconds of peace of mind."—Ralph Waldo Emerson

Peace of mind should be a priority in your life. Negative thoughts and feelings like anger, hatred, resentment, worry, and fear impact your peace of mind negatively. You can quiet your agitated and restless mind to overcome all worries, fears, anxieties, and stress.

How to have peace of mind:

- Engage in activities that take the mind away from its usual thoughts and worries;
- Avoid negative people and people that stress you out;
- Let go of ill feelings toward others by forgiving and forgetting;
- Accept things in your life that cannot be changed and move on;
- Don't let others make their problem your problem;
- Keep things in perspective;
- Take responsibility. Be accountable for your own actions and don't place blame on others;
- Apologize immediately whenever you do something wrong toward another;
- Be generous to others;
- Refrain from doing anything that will make you feel bad;
- Always give thanks for everything you have;

- Be patient;
- Choose your battles;
- Stay true to yourself. Be yourself and always do what you think is right;
- Slow down and remember that life is a journey, not a destination;
- Say no when your plate is full;
- Meditate and still your mind on a regular basis;
- Simplify your life;
- Devote time to relaxation on a regular basis;
- Do not let things beyond your control disrupt your peace of mind;
- Exercise on a regular basis;
- Pray for peace of mind.

Don't look to other people and things to give you peace; only you can give you peace.

A Great Time to be Alive

Like most things in life, aging is a state of mind, and you make it what it is. You mentally choose how you will age. You can choose to really live and not merely endure life. You can choose to age passionately, optimistically, and zealously, or you can choose to age with bitterness, depression, and despair. Like life in general, getting older isn't easy for most people. It can be. You can make the best of it and enjoy it. The secret to aging successfully is in how you perceive aging. Feel good about having survived mentally and physically in order to get to your age. Always be positive and always be thankful to be alive.

It's not what age you are, it's how you age that matters.

"Length of days *is* in her right hand*; and* in her left hand
riches and honour."—Proverbs 3:16

Age is not the passing of years, but the dawn of wisdom, substance, and increased spiritual power. Man has powers that transcend his physical powers. Wisdom is the awareness of the tremendous spiritual powers that we have within, and using these powers to lead a full and happy life. Aging should be a spiritual journey or a new phase of a spiritual journey. As you age spiritually, you grow spiritually. Focus more on connecting with others and finding new meaning in life. When you mature spiritually, you are able to use your spirituality to effectively deal with life's misfortunes. You are able to tap into your inner strength to cope with the proliferating loss of friends and family members, illness, diminished income, desolation, and despair that are sometimes associated with getting older.

"Dost thou love life? Then do not squander time, for that's the stuff life is made of."—Benjamin Franklin

There is a fountain of youth within you. Aging takes place in your mind. You create your own reality. You can stay young spiritually and thus, prolong the physical aspects of aging. It is essentially mind over matter. You primarily do this in the following ways: 1) avoiding and getting rid of fearful thoughts, since fearful thoughts create mental and physical decline; 2) living in the moment and not brooding over the past; 3) discovering and doing more things you love; 4) finding reasons to feel good; 5) always appreciating what you have; 6) not fearing death, and 7) acknowledging your eternalness.

"Life is a journey, not a destination" —Ralph Waldo Emerson

When some people grow old they lose interest in life, and they cease to dream. As you grow old, you should stay active and find new things to do. Do the things you always wanted to do but never had the time. Find things that make you happy. Travel. Learn a new hobby. Find something to be passionate about.

As you get older, you become more knowledgeable, more liberated, and stronger. Therefore, aging should be welcomed. It should be a time to search for new truths and new worlds to conquer. You can always learn new things, because your spirit never grows old. If you are not learning anything new, you are slowly dying.

It's never too late. Fall is just as lovely as Spring.

Growing old is a privilege. Aging is a gift of time and you need to use it to the fullest. Look for new sources of gratification and liveliness. Find what gives you a sense of worth and contentment. Stay open to new experiences, because through these experiences, your life will be enriched. Aging should be viewed as a new age of opportunities for fresh beginnings and fulfillment, not as spent youth.

"The fear of death follows from the fear of life. A man who lives fully is prepared to die at any time."—Mark Twain

Everything changes, transforms, and eventually passes away. We don't want to die, yet we don't want to be old. As we grow older, we become more mindful of our mortality and the finitude of life. Some people are afraid of getting older because they think they are getting closer to dying. It takes wisdom and courage to live a purposeful life while facing your mortality up close. It is only when you become conscious of death that you want to discover what life is truly about. When you are really cognizant of death is when you want to live your life to the fullest.

Don't be afraid of growing old. Time passes for everyone with no exceptions. Accept and prepare for change. Change will come. Being an older or old person is an unfamiliar and unique position to find oneself in. This is oftentimes disquieting, but it doesn't have to be. Appreciate that your outward beauty may fade, and your youthful body may deteriorate, but know that there is so much more to life than how you look. Although you must come to terms with the reality of your new self, you can stay young spiritually. Understand that as you grow older, and as you transcend the physical world to the spiritual world, life gratification increases respectively.

Age is relative. Life is measured by how well you live it, not how long you live it.

Dos and Don'ts of moving gracefully through time:
Do:

- Enjoy the simple things;
- Surround yourself with what you love;
- Accept the changes that inevitably come with aging;
- Exercise regularly;
- Eat healthy foods;
- Get plenty of sleep and relaxation;
- Be social. Don't isolate yourself from others;
- Get rid of stressors;
- Stay active;
- Be fabulous. Fix up and dress up;
- Love yourself;
- Do things that make you happy;
- Laugh a lot;

- Continue to do things you used to do, like listen to music;
- Be open to new experiences;
- Keep your independence;
- Tap into your youthful inner self;
- Strengthen your spiritual health;
- Appreciate being alive;
- Reflect on the positive aspects of aging;
- Endure grief and loss and get on with your life.

Don't:

- Dwell on the good ol' days
- Think about the negative aspects of aging;
- Feel sorry for yourself;
- Be afraid of getting older or growing old;
- Obsess about getting older or old;
- Focus on the physical aspects of aging;
- Age with a bad attitude;
- Stop learning;
- Mourn the loss of your youth or your beauty;
- Regret the past or worry about the future;
- Look for youth through another person;
- Smoke or drink excessively;
- Live vicariously through television shows. Live your own life instead.

Life After Life

We abhor death because we cannot bear to part with our friends and loved ones. We want to hold on to the past. We think that the past, with our loved ones in it, will never be surpassed in its virtue. Therefore after the death of a loved one, we wallow in the ruins of the past where we once felt comfort, love, and happiness. So we stay amongst the ruins as long as we can. In actuality, our loved ones are not dead. They are merely transformed, as the soul is eternal and omnipresent. Therefore, when a loved one dies we shouldn't grieve, but we should celebrate that person's life and be thankful that they were in our life for whatever period of time.

As we become aware of our own mortality, we often feel fear. This fear emanates from lack of knowledge. It is easy to accept death when you understand that death is a natural extension of living and that death is a part of spiritual evolution. It is widely believed that when we die, our physical bodies cease to exist and our life-sustaining energy is released back into the universe, but our souls survive. In other words, death is simply the detachment of our body and our soul. Therefore, the demise of the physical body does not terminate the essence of life. In fact, death is merely a transition from one body to another.

It is believed that one's spiritual and mental state at the time of death is extremely important, as it can be empowering. If you are in a state of acceptance and surrender yourself to God, your transition to another plane of existence will be undertaken positively. Remember that death of the physical body does not terminate the consciousness, as it is eternal.

Many are unaware that there is life after life. An unborn child in its mother's womb probably thinks that the womb is all there is to life, and thus it is unaware that there is life after birth. Like an unborn child is born to live life in the world as we know it, we die in order to live again in another reality. Dying is part of living. The cycle of creation is birth, life, and death. If we believe this cycle of creation exists, then we must believe we are reborn after we die. This means that our bodies may die, but the soul (energy) within us never dies, as energy is infinite. As spiritual beings, the pure essence of our being cannot be destroyed. It just changes form. Therefore we will always exist.

The caterpillar: "I thought I had died, but I had turned into a butterfly."

Scholars and philosophers have defined this as reincarnation, which is the belief that the soul is reborn in physical bodies again and again. The underlying premise is that the soul comes back to learn the lessons that were not learned the previous times. That is, we are given as many opportunities as it takes to return to the physical world for lessons that lead to spiritual maturity. Thus, we are given as many lifetimes as we need to grow and evolve into enlightened souls. Our life's journey includes life tests, which are lessons that we must all learn in order to become enlightened. Our souls reach a level of enlightenment when we master the lessons we are here to learn. The mastery of these lessons determines how quickly the soul advances on the spiritual path, and how many times it must be reborn on the earth to learn these life lessons.

Once we have evolved into the ultimate beings, we do not need to return. However, some highly evolved souls may choose to be reincarnated, for the purpose of helping and teaching others to evolve spiritually. Others will be reincarnated to settle their karmic accounts. The law of karma and the law of cause and effect are synonymous, except the law of karma advocates that the effect may be in the present lifetime or the next lifetime. Accordingly, a person's intentions and actions not only affect a person's current life, but future lives as well. Therefore, one may return to atone for past bad deeds. This atonement, however, is not for the purpose of punishment. It is for the purpose of learning. The law of karma principally asserts we are reborn for the purpose of learning myriad lessons in our personal evolution. We keep developing until we have reached a higher dimensional state, a state where negative karma no longer exists.

Although our soul remains unchanged when we reincarnate, our personality changes. We do carry over some personality traits from our previous existence in the physical world, however. The spiritual state of being we evolved to in the physical world is the spiritual state we take with us.

I possessed only a superficial belief in reincarnation until I personally had a past life awareness experience. As a result of copious twists and turns on my life journey, I found myself living in London, England. While living there, I always felt a sense of belonging and a poignant sense of having lived there before. Everywhere I went I felt an intense sense of familiarity. One night, while I was awake in a relaxed state, I saw a vision of two Englishmen in their sixties on bikes on a road in the countryside. I could see them and hear them as though I were watching a movie, yet I could feel that one of the men was me. When he spoke, it was as though I were speaking. It is very hard to explain, but I knew immediately that it was not a dream, but a replay of an experience in a past life. I felt both elated and a little freaked out. Of course whenever I share this with anyone, their reaction is one of disbelief and they assume that I was dreaming. This was without a doubt not a dream.

Play to Win

Getting what you want:

Firstly, you must claim what you want;
Secondly, you must have a strong desire for the thing or event;
Thirdly, you must have the faith and belief that you can have the thing or that the event can happen;
Fourthly, you must believe in the power of your subconscious mind to manifest the thing or event without any doubt whatsoever;
Fifthly, you must visualize the thing or event.
Then, you must act on it, if necessary.

Being happy:

Make enjoyment of life a priority. Enjoyment should not be a reward and not something to be put off until some event takes place. Every day of your life, find something to enjoy. You will find that your life is more balanced and productive. Do what makes you happy. This does not necessarily refer to your life's work or your occupation. It refers to everyday living. If playing with your grandchild makes you happy, play with your grandchild every chance you get. If a nature walk makes you happy, do it on a regular basis. If writing a poem gives you pleasure, write lots of poems! Doing what gives you joy and pleasure will put you in a state of happiness. You will feel happy, and this will create thoughts of happiness and other positive thoughts, which in turn will draw more good things to you.

Finding peace of mind:

It isn't what you have, or where you live, or who you are that gives you peace of mind. It's how you feel and your reaction to life and its challenges that give you peace of mind. Although peace of mind is only found within, it helps to free yourself from environments, circumstances, and people that upset you. You must also free yourself from negative thoughts and feelings. Moreover, once you understand and embrace the relationship between your spirit soul and the universe (God), you will be closer to attaining peace of mind.

Go big or go home:

It is believed that this phrase originated as a product slogan for a motorcycle exhaust system in the 1990s. The slogan has gained in popularity, and generally means play to win or don't play. Another interpretation describes the code of champions: You have to play hard to win or you'll go home as losers. It is also used to motivate people to give it their all. My own personal interpretation means to go all the way and do whatever you do to its fullest and best. Follow the laws of the universe and do not let fear keep you from achieving your goals and dreams.

It's all good, all the time:

Always know and believe that no matter what challenges you may face in life, it's going to be okay. All challenges are temporary. Furthermore, because we are one with the universe (God), and the source of our power is within us, life is always good despite these temporary challenges.

Accept and believe:

- That you live and exist in what is referred to as an infinite mind, and you create with your mind.
- Your life is a manifestation of your thinking, as you create your physical world through your thoughts.

- The power of your infinite mind will guide and direct you spiritually, mentally, and materially.
- You have the power to think as you choose.
- You have the power and the right to change your thinking if you do not like the results of your current thinking. Ergo, you have the power to change negative detrimental thoughts into positive thoughts in order to change something in your physical life.
- You can change your life by changing your thoughts, beliefs and feelings.
- In all circumstances, you can think your way out of troubles.
- There is a single universal consciousness from which all things manifest, and our individual minds are a part of this universal mind.
- God created this world and these universal laws to govern this world. When you understand and follow these laws you receive divine benefit from them.
- We are universal in nature. We are all *one* and we are interconnected to everyone and everything else in existence.
- It is love that holds the universe together, and the more we love the closer we are to God the creator.
- We can evolve spiritually into a supreme essence in our consciousness.
- Nothing happens by chance. Every effect has a preceding cause.
- In thinking good of another, you are actually thinking good of yourself. In thinking ill of another, you are actually thinking ill of yourself.
- If you care about others and bless others, you will be blessed.
- If you give as you hope to receive, whatever you give will be given back to you.
- Love, compassion, and acceptance are what life is all about, and it is precisely what keeps us existing.
- Spiritual love is the ultimate lesson we are in the physical world to learn. Life is about loving everything and everyone in the universe and not about loving material things.
- Loving others is not sufficient; you must manifest love, teach, and serve others.

- Gratitude will give you more goodness in your life and enhance everything that is good.
- Whatever you want most in life, you will attain by giving it to someone else first.
- How you live your present life will determine what kind of future (reincarnated) life you will have.

Life To-Do List:

- Be attentive and appreciative on a constant basis of how much you've been given.
- Believe, believe, believe! Believe both in the thing or condition, and believe in the power of the infinite mind within you.
- Explore the many facets of life and really live them all by pursuing life with fervor.
- Live life as a journey and not a destination.
- Always trade despair for hope, fear for courage, depression for happiness, and resentment for love.
- Constantly feed your mind with positive thoughts.
- Make daily affirmations. Read or say them aloud several times a day.
- Always express gratitude. Upon awakening in the morning, reflect on your life and express gratitude for all you have and all the good in your life.
- Handle your business. Remember: proper planning and preparation prevents piss-poor performance.
- Always try to turn lemons into lemonade. Ask yourself, "How can I make the best of a bad situation?"
- Help others with broken hearts, broken dreams, and broken spirits, as this will help you.
- Live in accordance with *oneness*, and do not prevent others from reaching their divine potential to the fullest.
- Remember: the things you take for granted, someone else is praying for.
- Remind yourself during hard times that they won't last forever and that they are only temporary.
- Express the God in you, and manifest God to everyone around you.
- Serve others without expectation of something in return.
- Forgive others unconditionally.
- Always make your relationships with others more important than any issues you may have with them.
- Pursue happiness.
- Follow through with actions to make your dreams materialize.

- Expect success.
- Replace "I can't" thoughts with "I can" thoughts.
- Learn from your mistakes and failures.
- Look within yourself, to your infinite power and wisdom to solve your problems.
- Meditate daily.
- Listen to your inner voice.
- Make the last thoughts before falling asleep, positive thoughts.

Life Don't-Do List:

- Don't hold negative thoughts, such as doubt, fear, hatred, and resentment.
- Don't suffer negative conditions.
- Don't have negative people in your life.
- Don't judge others.
- Don't let the past hold you captive. Let it go.
- Don't use the past as an excuse for your unfavorable circumstances and conditions in life.
- Don't be afraid to fail or succeed.
- Don't let criticism of you by others affect you negatively.
- Don't run from your problems and troubles.
- Don't see yourself as a victim. Victims blame others, feel sorry for themselves, refuse to take responsibility, and believes the world owes them something.
- Don't focus on what you don't have. Focus on what you do have.
- Don't hold thoughts that make you feel bad, as you will attract more bad things to you.
- Don't wait for things to happen. Make them happen.
- Don't ever give up on becoming who you want to be.
- Don't repay evil with evil.
- Don't forget to laugh.

Notes to Self:

- Thought allows us to model the world we experience. I create a perfect world with perfect thoughts.
- When I believe and affirm that I can have the life I want, I can have it.
- Success comes to those who believe in the power of mind.
- The more I affirm what I want, the more of it I will get.
- The greater the gratitude expressed, the greater the abundance I will receive.
- Everyone makes mistakes, and people are not to be defined by their mistakes.
- Success comes to those who believe in the power of the mind and who think deeply and persistently about their success.
- If I think I can't do something, I can't.
- I fail if I don't try.
- I attract what I fear.
- Courage is not the absence of fear; it is facing my fears and acting positively in spite of my fear.
- If I offend or attack another person, I cannot gain their good will, as everyone wants to be loved and appreciated, and made to feel important.
- When I blame others, my problem doesn't go away, it perpetuates.
- Persistent anger will make me bitter and resentful.
- Negative situations and people will continue to come into my life if I do not learn the lesson regarding negative feelings like, hatred, resentment, fear, guilt, and worry.
- In order for me to be forgiven, I must forgive others.
- To hope is to dream of a better future. If I give up hope I lose.
- The stars don't shine without darkness.
- I will accept others as they are, without judgment.
- When I rise above fear, I open myself to unconditional love.
- I will treat others as I want to be treated.
- I am my brother, and my brother is me.
- I will give as I hope to receive.
- The key to a long and successful life is loving people and not loving material things.

- Life is a gift, and growing old is a privilege.
- The key to successful aging is accepting the changes that go along with it.
- I don't have to be young to decide to be successful.
- I'm never too old to stop learning.
- Life involves constantly leaving something or someone behind.
- When I am in a state of happiness, my positive thoughts and feelings will attract good things to me.
- Positive thoughts are more powerful than negative thoughts.
- The difference between dreams and reality is action.
- Leading a happy, well-balanced life is a priority in my life.
- I will focus on the journey, not the destination.
- I can always find something to be thankful for.
- Gratitude activates the law of attraction, therefore I will be grateful for what I want.
- Struggle makes me stronger.
- The pathway to enlightenment is strewn with suffering, and to get past it, I have to endure.
- In the end, it's not the years in my life that count; it's the life in my years.

Final Thoughts:

Forgive *everyone*;
Judge *no one*;
Love *everyone*.

"Before I act, I will *listen*.
Before I react, I will *think*.
Before I spend, I will *earn*.
Before I criticize, I will *wait*.
Before I pray, I will *forgive*.
Before I quit, I will *try*." —Unknown

"Everything will be okay in the end. If it's not okay, it's not the end."—Unknown

Sample Affirmations

Affirmations are positive statements made in the present tense to assert that something is so.

1. I am at peace. The peace of the universe controls my heart.
2. I attract good fortune to myself, as I rejoice in the success and good fortune of others.
3. I am a valuable, loving, and giving person, and I deserve and receive happiness and prosperity.
4. I expect the best at all times.
5. I am free.
6. I am blessed.
7. God is my refuge and strength, an ever present help.
8. I am of good courage and strength, for my God is with me wherever I go.
9. My business is abundantly profitable.
10. I am healthy, wealthy, wise, beautiful, and fit.
11. I let go of the past, and I look forward to the future, as it is a wonderful new beginning for me.
12. I live a full and bountiful life.
13. The spirit of truth is within me, and guides me in all things.
14. Within me is the power to attain enduring wealth and prosperity.
15. I am filled with energy, every day.
16. I am whole, perfect, strong, powerful, loving, happy, and at peace.
17. Infinite intelligence is within me and guides and directs me.
18. Every project that I endeavor is successful.
19. My subconscious mind helps me prosper spiritually, mentally, and materially.

20. Perfect health is mine, and my body works in perfect harmony.
21. Beauty, love, peace, and abundance are mine, right now.
22. Divine order governs my entire life.
23. I can do all things through the power of my subconscious mind.
24. I am the master of my fate.
25. I believe in good fortune, divine guidance, and the power of creativity.
26. All the blessings of life are mine now.
27. I believe in the power of my mind to create my perfect reality.
28. I can endure all things.
29. I trust myself and I have confidence in myself.
30. I have the unfading beauty of a gentle and quiet spirit.
31. I ask; I expect to receive; I receive.
32. I focus on positive outcomes and I receive positive outcomes.
33. I put my trust in God, and everything I pray for is fulfilled.
34. I have the strength within me to handle anything.
35. I dwell in safety, and I lie down and sleep in peace.
36. I believe, and I receive.
37. Everything is possible.
38. When one door closes, another one always opens.
39. I find comfort in knowing I am armed with strength, and my way is made perfect.
40. I am encouraged, and I have hope for a better life.
41. It's all good all the time.
42. My life is enhanced in many wonderful ways when I show charity and goodwill toward others.
43. I expect a miracle.
44. I have plenty, and I am content.
45. I am filled with love, joy, peace, patience, kindness, goodness, faithfulness, gentleness, and self-control.
46. I fight the good fight, and I finish the race.
47. I grow in wisdom every day.
48. I think only good thoughts of those who have wronged me.
49. I am kind and compassionate to everyone; I love everyone, and I forgive everyone.
50. I soar on wings like eagles do. I run and do not grow weary.
51. I choose happiness.

Inspired Writings

The Way Was Rough

The way was rough
through both darkness and light,
full of pitfalls and snares.
But through it all we relied on His might.

Holding steadfast to our faith,
as we saw trouble both bitter and rare -
Because of our faith in the Lord,
we were always sure of how we would fare.

With hope and courage -
Never did we fear.
And so we persevered,
for we knew success would be near.

It was an uphill climb all the way through -
Fraught with trials and suffering, to be sure.
It was our faith and belief,
that showed us how to endure.

It's been a long and arduous road,
but it has come to an end.
The road forks,
so we'll turn and start again.

Fallen Angel

Fallen angel -
How far did you fall?
Your harshness belies you.
Did you not fulfill your call?

Fallen angel -
Where have you been?
Your wings are singed and broken.
How did you sin?

Your smile of grace reaches,
touching soul to soul.
I cry for you -
For your dishonor untold.

A terrestrial enigma you are.
Your kindness transcends inimitable pain.
Though your intrinsic beauty possesses piety,
Sanctity you could not regain.

Entwined in a celestial storm -
To strangers you show love.
Your essence calms them -
Like the equanimity of a dove.

Fallen angel -
You can regain your sovereignty.
Be strong and take heart.
Forgotten will be your iniquity.

Swept Away

Swept away by the winds of anger -
With nothing to hold on to.
Seeing no goodness, only danger,
Danger not true.

Swept away, like the past -
The pain and agony you try to blot out.
The present you ignore -
While forgetting what life is about.

Swept away like a hurricane -
Tearing through with no hope.
Thinking of nothing -
Except, "How will I cope?"

Like a hurricane -
Whose rage is unleashed
on unsuspecting victims,
You wonder, "When will it cease?"

After the hurricane,
and the turmoil is past -
only self-pity remains,
and a die has been cast.

Not knowing,
He is a portent to many.
If you'll just hold on -
Your cup he will fill with plenty.

Clouds

As I stand here and I gaze
up at the clouds above,
They remind me of happier days -
Filled only with joy and love.

The clouds enclose me.
Reminiscent of majesty,
they take me away,
Far away in a reverie.

I think of days gone by,
and wonder if they are gone forever -
Or merely stored in the clouds,
and there held quietly, forever and ever.

Take the time to look at the clouds,
when you feel sad and low.
Then retrieve your memories from the clouds -
Your joy and happiness, again you will know.

A reflection of your soul
in the clouds you'll also see.
The closer you look, the more you'll see -
Shrouded in grace and mystery.

Clouds tell stories of long ago,
with their rhythm and blues.
Look deeper and deeper, there you will find truth,
As secrets are hidden in their many hues.

Clouds can fill you with reverence
for the almighty up above.
Sometimes they fill you with foreboding,
But usually a peaceful and serene love.

How Can You Judge Me?

You don't know me,
or where I've been.
So, how can you judge me -
Or my heart within?

You look at me
with enmity.
You do not see
but a reflection of infamy.

You think you know me -
I feel your contempt.
How can you judge me?
Is your soul exempt?

You can't understand me,
unless you get into my head.
Please do not judge me -
Seek edification instead.

Sagacious or foolish?
How could you know?
You think yourself more worthy,
And you dare to loathe.

With platitudes you speak of me -
As though I don't exist.
You ridicule and taunt me,
and my dire predicament.

How can you judge -
That which you do not understand?
Yourself, you do not judge.
Before God's judgment seat we will all stand.

If you could walk in my shoes
through my egregious past -
Not judging, but learning,
maybe you'd understand me at last.

Your sanctity astounds me.
You judge me culpable at best.
Judging by mere appearances -
Condemning and forgetting the rest.

Why do you look down on me?
Do not judge me, your brother.
There is only one judge.
There is no other.

If you would judge yourself -
You would not judge another.
If you judge others, so you will be judged –
Do not look down on your brother.

A Beacon

Life: sometimes dark, sometimes bright,
like a beacon that flashes off and on.
Sometimes short, sometimes long.
A hand reached out in a storm.

The purpose? To guide
other connected souls,
To be there for them,
And to lift them from their lows.

Let our lights join,
touching light to light -
Soul to soul,
revealing all His might.

May joy and laughter radiate from your light,
overtaking shadows of doubts and fear.
May passion and courage displace fright
in the knowledge that the Lord is near.

To guide out of the depths,
those that have fallen so deep –
To lift them up toward eternity -
It is His light that shines so steep.

Light that shines like a flash of lightning -
Clearing the path of troubles and pain.
Light for those who dwell in darkness,
granting a powerful spirit to sustain.

The Beginning of the End

It's the beginning
of the end, I see.
Where before there was nothing,
suddenly everything is clear to me.

The end of the road
called misery,
That I've trod for so long,
will soon be a distant memory.

My sorrow is gone!
My burden is now light,
for a weight has been lifted.
Now I know the end is in sight.

Happiness eluded me -
Before I could not see.
I thank God for my blessings
and for the end of my misery.

Filled with hopes of a new beginning -
I can see; now my path is bright.
The only question—
Do I turn left or right?

Mistakes

Mistakes are consequences of lessons
we failed to learn before.
So face them and conquer them,
or they will come again, more, and more, and more.

Life is short and precious -
With many victories yet to be won.
Learn your lessons quickly –
Prosper and move on.

Mistakes mean promises like,
"I'll never do it again."
So where you made a mistake before -
Next time knowledge and wisdom should win.

If you ignore your mistakes -
It will bring suffering and pain.
With knowledge and wisdom
there is a lot to gain.

To make a mistake
is not a punishable sin –
And not to be shamed -
But a means of finding your power within.

If Only I Knew

If only I knew who
rescued me from the treacherous sea -
Pulling me out of the swells
of the deep waters of iniquity.

If only I knew why
His angels alighted, lifting me
up to His empyreal realm -
Though at first I could not see.

If only I knew God
when His glory opened my eyes, and -
I could see His majesty,
as I took the outstretched hand.

If only I knew when
He wiped away the tears,
and gave me new life -
That gone were the sad and lonely years.

If only I knew how
To make jubilant and joyful times not few.
The hardships not endless -
Things would have been easier, if only I knew.

If only I knew before
that God's grace will come -
Only after believing the esoteric truth -
That the battle will be won.

Whoever lives and believes in Him -
I now know -
Will never die,
but his spirit will continue to grow.

I know why -
When I look back on my life.
It is a quandary, but I do not ponder
my trials, tribulations and strife.

Always Tomorrow

The first day of the beginning
is always tomorrow.
Look forward to it with zeal
and forget about today's strife and sorrow.

You can always start
your life over again.
There is always tomorrow -
Yet another chance to win.

Lack of faith and courage
will hold you back -
With resolution and ardor,
get your life back on track.

After night is always the day.
After the heartache, the pain, the grief,
The disillusionment, sadness, and dismay –
With each new day, a chance for joy and relief.

Tomorrow comes like the spring.
After winter, always it comes.
Forget about the past.
You will wake up to many new suns.

When the sun goes down,
let it set on the problems of the day.
Look forward to the new dawn -
Trust God; He will show you the way.

Peace of Mind

Whenever your spirit resides in peace -
You will find peace that will last.
Therefore, set your heart free -
Start by letting go of the past.

Let the spirit of truth be your guide.
Look only for the good in everything.
If what you seek is of the Divine -
The bell of victory will triumphantly ring.

God grants all desires.
Always expect only the best.
Rely on his infinite power.
Expect less, and you'll receive less.

By showing forgiveness and mercy to us,
Forgiveness and mercy our Father does teach.
When you give forgiveness freely,
Inner peace you can reach.

Show charity and good will to others
In all your days.
Be kind to your brothers –
It will return to you in many ways.

Show love by giving from the heart,
and you will receive it in kind.
Share with those who are in need.
Then you will find true peace of mind.

In Exile Is Where I've Been

In exile is where I've been—
it was cold, lonely, and bleak.
A pseudo-abode,
no place for the timid or weak.

Like one who abdicates the throne,
I gave up all that was dear to me.
My family, my friends, my home,
my crown a mere memory.

I used my prowess and skill
to survive in a wilderness of the unknown.
And I stay there until—
until I'm free to go home.

I dream of home both night and day
while I wait to emancipate.
My hopes ephemeral,
always wondering: will I awake?

A prodigious sadness
becomes a part of me.
I walk the streets forlorn
as my exile seems to stretch to infinity.

But in the panorama of life
I see behind me an end—
a cornucopia of experience.
In exile is where I've been.

Infinity

Glorious splendor of His majesty—
boundless and endless love.
Forever and ever it is yours,
as he showers his grace from above.

When you think that He cares no more,
He lifts you up into his arms—
protects you and cares for you,
and to you will come no harm.

His forgiveness is ceaseless,
His power sublime.
He yearns for your closeness,
His mercy boundless in time.

Forsake you, He will not,
for his love is divine.
He is there as your refuge—
now, and throughout time.

Like His word, stretching to infinity,
His promises He will keep.
Forever and ever,
His blessings you will reap.

Look in Their Eyes

Look in their eyes,
and there you'll see.
In shades of gray—
despair and misery.

A reflection of an abyss,
deep down you'll see.
Standing on the precipice of hopelessness
and wretchedness so steep.

With distant looks,
they dream afar;
wondering if their pain will ever leave—
Les Misérables is what they are.

Their eyes are hollow,
with no hint of peace;
Hoping
everyday their suffering will cease.

No relief in sight,
none they see.
Thinking only of their plight
and their misery.

Help them, console them,
be with them, I say.
Pull them back from the precipice;
Lord have mercy on them, I pray.

What Can I Say?

What can I say?
I don't have much.
Because you do have little—
you can say, "Thank you so much."

Why do you complain
because you don't have riches and such?
Since you do have life,
you can say, "Thank you so much."

Why don't you appreciate?
Why can't you see?
Why can't you say, "Thank you so much"
for the blessings He has given free?

You asked for His help
when you were needy and sad.
You forgot about His blessings—
never appreciating what you had.

One day, you'll see—
because you didn't appreciate—
as he gave them to you—
He takes your blessings away.

When He takes the rain away—
you will remember the Sun.
When He takes the Sun away—
you will recall what you should have done.

Give thanks to Him
in all circumstance.
Praise His name in thanks,
while you have the chance.

The Eyes

From sullen pools
the tears do not efface.
The weariness of years,
that only providence can erase.

Barren and cold, disheartened
as they search for the egress.
From their prison of scorn,
that no retribution can redress.

Searching for understanding
of life's mysteries.
Reaching for resolutions;
hoping for life's small victories.

No exultation to be seen.
Happiness, the eyes elude.
Unveiling suffering and pain—
only sadness they exude.

One day I know,
the eyes will see—
Happiness, peace, and love.
Life is no longer a cruel effigy.

Lord Have Mercy on Me

When I am feeling discouraged
and life weighs heavy on me.
I sigh and I say,
"Lord have mercy on me."

Oh, my soul,
why do you despair?
You know God is with you—
in you, around, and even in the air.

You do not have to worry;
it's time for you to be strong.
God will forgive
all you've done wrong.

If it's mercy you look for,
long you will not wait.
No other can compare,
as His power is great.

His mercy he will give you,
even if you are meek.
His compassion will find you,
if only you seek.

I sigh and I say,
"Lord have mercy," again.
I feel better just saying it—
as He washes away my sorrow within.

Kind and Gentle Soul

Unbeknownst to all,
like a thief in the night—
you move with stealth,
not to show your light.

Your value—
it is hard to measure.
Not vermeil, nor fool's gold,
you are one of God's treasures

Encased in a shell of granite and stone—
if only your story could be told.
Truly a wonder to behold.
May God bless your kind and gentle soul.

All will know,
what a stellar gift you are.
God will shower his grace on you,
and the light of your soul will shine far.

He Will See You Through It All

When your thoughts trouble you,
and you are distraught;
when suffering is upon you,
and you feel your life is worth naught,

When you feel downtrodden and alone;
when fear grips you like steel,
and you don't know which way to turn;
when heartache is all too real,

Live by faith!
Though you cannot see,
remember, He will be with you.
Let go, and let it be.

Soon you will not be troubled.
Neither will you be afraid.
Trust in Him, your Lord.
He will surely come to your aid.

Be at peace with God.
He transcends all.
Wait for Him in your heart.
Wait, he will heed your call.

Though you stumble,
you will not fall.
As your everlasting shepherd,
He will see you through it all.

Never Alone

I was never alone—
for he was with me, you see.
Out of the pit and up on a stone—
His angels watched over me.

For I praised him all day long—
never would he let me perish.
In body, mind, and soul—
His faithfulness I will always cherish

I felt lonely at times—
and I thought, on my own.
But his spirit was inside me—
so I was never alone.

I put my trust in Him—
Though I could not see.
Stepping out on faith—
it was more than just me.

It was by His grace,
that my fear would cease.
I'm strong and triumphant,
and finally at peace.

He Tested Us

With dishonor and regret,
we were driven away.
Into the tunnel of plaintiveness—
prostate we waited in dismay.

On our knees reverently—
we stumbled and crawled about.
No egress could we find—
errantly we looked for a way out.

Through fire and water
we plod along in disgrace.
Abundance and prosperity—
hunger and afflictions did displace.

The burdens were many.
Travesty trod us like a horse
gone wild, stomping out infamy.
Through hardship and infelicity we stayed the course.

We lost everything—
even our beds.
Yet our faith was not shaken—
though tigers and lions clawed at our heads.

After much arduous strife,
He returned our dignity—
and gave us back our life,
with renewed abundance and prosperity.

What a capacious test to pass—
with steep slopes and summits to transcend.
Our tenacity we knew had to last—
so that we might win in the end.

After testing us, again and again—
our prize—His everlasting love—
exultation and blessings,
bestowed on us from above.

Here

My heart is heavy,
and I am in pain.
But I don't worry,
for tomorrow I will try again.

Each day is a challenge—
I look forward to the night—
where peace and serenity
have not taken flight.

The next morning I start all over—
thinking of my plight.
Memories plague me and hover—
until the next night.

My surroundings oppress me,
but I will not fear—
for I am filled with joyful thoughts
of one day leaving here.

I will leave this experience in the past.
I'll only look forward with joy and glee.
I'll be glad these days
are far behind me.

I look forward to the day
when here is a distant memory.
The tears I cry, I'll wipe away
and not make them a part of me.

Elena

She came from afar,
her dreams naïve.
Searching for that elusive star
many tried to deceive.

She does not show off her quiet might.
The truth be told—
she is cunning and bright.
Her strength, behold!

Her compassionate side is seen more often than not.
You can find comfort in her, if it's comfort you seek.
If you step on her toes she will set you straight,
a pillar of strength for the timid and weak.

In reaching for the prize, it moves beyond her reach.
It's an uphill climb that she knows she will win.
When she gets discouraged
She rests, then says, "Let's start again."

She believes in the Lord with body and soul.
I bid her farewell and peace from above.
Her delightful spirit is a sight to behold.
I pray she will fly home on the wings of Love.

Life Is But a Whisper in Time

Barely felt and barely heard—
life is but a whisper in time.
A portentous truth, if unknown,
like the tinkling of a chime.

Love life and live life,
as life is sublime.
To love life is to love God.
Moment by moment be aware of time.

Live this life now.
Do not dwell in the past.
We are not here for long.
Now—a reality that will not last.

Suffer, endure, understand, care.
Climb high, dive deep, rise above.
Change, conquer, achieve, dare.
Smell, touch, laugh, love.

Live and know life in its many facets.
Let living be a lesson and a fine art.
The future will reward you with plenty.
Pursue life with a fearless and fervent heart.

Evanescent dreams, a brevity
in life's uncertain chapters.
A short journey to destiny.
In the end, only the journey matters.

What Hope Is All About

The waves were rough
on that interminable sea.
We looked for land;
no land could we see.

We had hopes of finding land,
before it was too late.
We were determined not to give up.
For God's miracles we'd wait.

Despair blew through
like a cold North wind—
But our trust in the Lord
gave us hope in the end.

We waited patiently for the winds to change.
We waited for what seemed like an eternity.
Just as we were about to give up hope,
we said, "Is that land that we see?"

It was land that we saw— –
land without a doubt.
Never give up—
That's what hope is all about.

CPSIA information can be obtained at www.ICGtesting.com
Printed in the USA
LVOW10s0703251015

459639LV00001B/10/P